TEROA

The Enigmatic Realms of Ashcroft

The Enigmatic Realms of Ashcroft

Reid Abraxas

Copyright © 2023 by Reid Abraxas

All rights reserved.

No part of this publication may be reproduced, distributed, or transmitted in any form or by any means, including photocopying, recording, or other electronic or mechanical methods, without the prior written permission of the publisher, except as permitted by U.S. copyright law. For permission requests, contact Rabraxas13@protonmail.com

The story, all names, characters, and incidents portrayed in this production are fictitious. No identification with actual persons (living or deceased), places, buildings, and products is intended or should be inferred.

Book Cover by R.A.

First edition 2023

Dedications

You are the light in my life and now we are just a couple of peas in a pod. I love you dearly. Thank you for always being there even in my darkest times.

I have always cherished the memories of our bedtime stories; from the Velveteen Rabbit, to Three Billy Goats Gruff, and everything in between. Honk, Beep, Squeak, and Peep. It was maybe the only thing that helped turn the tide when all seemed against me. Stories and fond memories are all we have to hold on to in seas of uncertainty.

Table Of Contents

Chapter 1: The Ephemeral Echoes 7-11

Chapter 2: A Maze of Light and Shadow 12-13

Chapter 3: The Echoes of Elysium 14-17

Chapter 4: Endless Alcove 18-21

Chapter 5: The Dreamers Descent 22-26

Chapter 6: In The Company of Shadows 27-30

Chapter 7: The Quest for Shadow 31-35

Chapter 8: The Bridge Between Dreams 36-39

Chapter 9: Tower Obsidian 40-47

Chapter 10: Resonance of Reverie 48-56

Chapter 11: Resonance of Dreams 57-61

Chapter 12: Veil Of Shadows 62-79

Chapter 14: Carnival Of Shadows 80-89

Chapter 15: The Great Tapestry 90-92

TEROA

The Enigmatic Realms of Ashcroft

Chapter 1: The Ephemeral Echoes

The air in Wicklow was dense with an ethereal mist, a silvery haze that rendered the quaint town almost phantasmal. In the cold, somber heart of that spectral fog, an ancient mansion stood, its timeworn stones whispering secrets of bygone eras. It was known as the Ashcroft Estate, a name that elicited a shiver down the spines of the most stoic souls.

I, Rhineheart, had only just arrived, drawn by the rumors that darted about like hushed murmurs in the wind—of an uncanny phenomenon enveloping the estate. Yet, as I stood before its majestic facade, it was not just the mystery that beckoned; it was the siren call of legacy, a potent allure that had ensnared countless souls before me.

It was said that within the echoing chambers of Ashcroft, one could hear the fading memories of its occupants, whispers of those who had come and gone, striving to etch their mark upon the annals of time. A soft rustling, like old pages turning, wafted through the ebon tendrils of night as I ventured toward the mansion.

Perched atop a gentle rise, the Ashcroft Estate cut an imposing figure against the horizon. Its architecture was a seamless blend of Gothic Revival and Victorian styles, a monument in and of itself to the tastes of its original builders and the eras they spanned. The main building was a sprawling three-story manor, constructed from grayish-blue stones that had been meticulously quarried and shaped to fit together perfectly. Over time, ivy had started to creep up its walls, lending an age-old charm to its external image.

The estate's large windows, arched at the top, were adorned with intricate leaded glass, the kind seen in ancient cathedrals or structures of antiquity. These windows not only provided glimpses into the opulence within, but also reflected the vast landscape surrounding the manor, making the building appear as if it was a part of the very earth it stood upon.

The main entrance was marked by a massive stained glass door, studded with iron and oak, roots of a tree seemed to grow through and within the glass as if the building was alive . On either side of the entrance pathway were tall, symmetrical gas lamps; aglow with the warmth of moonlit fire, creating a welcoming yet foreboding atmosphere.

As I entered through the ornate glass door, the words of many coalesced into a symphony, tales of valor and heartache, ambition and desolation. It was evident that the line between the present and the past had blurred, the stories merging, forming a poignant tapestry of lives lived, dreams pursued, and legacies yearned for.

"Legacy," I mused, the word tasting bittersweet upon my tongue. "The indelible impression one leaves behind, the vestige that resists the inexorable march of time."

Yet, as I would soon discern, along with many others drawn to this enigma, Ashcroft's tale was not just one of ghostly echoes or forgotten myths. It was an ode to the enduring spirit, a witness to the undying need to be remembered. Through its elusive mysteries, many would come to understand the profound importance of leaving behind something greater than oneself, an eternal echo that would resonate through the ages.

The true story of Ashcroft was not merely of walls and whispers, but of the perennial human quest: to forge a legacy that defies the fleeting nature of existence.

And as the sun's first rays pierced the mist, casting reddish light through the stain-glassed windows, I felt a renewed determination. I would unravel the enigma of Ashcroft, and in doing so, perhaps discover the essence of my own legacy.

Inside, the mansion revealed a paradoxical blend of opulence and decay. Gilded mirrors and ornate chandeliers bore witness to better days, while mildewed drapes and cracked marble hinted at years of neglect. But despite its forlorn appearance, there was an indomitable aura that permeated every nook and cranny—an indistinct energy that seemed both ancient and very much alive.

As I ambled, I encountered other wanderers, each drawn to Ashcroft with a sense of purpose, albeit obscured; while exploring the main halls, I noticed from the periphery of my vision, as if appearing out of thin air, Clarissa, with cerulean eyes that seemed to have pierced the depths of many souls; and Adolwolf, as I would soon realize, a scholar with an insatiable curiosity, always found with a tome in one hand and a magnifying glass in the other.

Clarissa stood at a medium height, her stature exuding an air of quiet confidence. Her skin was a soft alabaster, almost luminescent under certain lights, contrasted starkly by her blond hair streaked with auburn strands, cascading down her back in soft waves.

Her eyes were perhaps her most striking feature: a deep shade of emerald green and cerulean blue, they seemed to harbor secrets, stories, and emotions, capable of captivating anyone who dared to look into them for too long. Framed by long, dark lashes, her eyes had a way of expressing her feelings even when she said nothing.

Adolwolf was tall, his height accentuated further by his impeccable posture. With broad shoulders, he conveyed an aura of strength and vitality but tempered through wisdom. Dressed with meticulous care, he had a preference for dark, tailored suits that complemented his physique. The only consistent accessory was a vintage pocket watch, passed down through generations, which he often consulted, not to tell time but as if seeking counsel from the past.

I introduced myself, but could not shake the feeling that we were familiar with one another, as if we had each forgotten old friends. As we conversed, a door creaked open somewhere above the main hall, and a zephyr imbued with hints of lavender and old parchment wafted through. It was as if the mansion itself was beckoning us closer, urging us to unravel its many mysterious. As the three of us ventured upwards, the ambiance grew denser, charged with anticipation. Each step on the groaning staircase seemed to echo with a mélange of laughter, tears, and fervent conversations from ages past.

The further we delved, the more apparent it became that Ashcroft wasn't merely a passive witness. There was an alchemical transformation at work, where past legacies merged with present aspirations, where forgotten dreams found new voice, and where every seeker, including myself, was gently nudged towards a greater understanding of what it meant to truly leave a lasting mark.

The mystery deepened as we explored. And as the shadows lengthened, the mansion whispered its truths, awaiting the moment of epiphany when each of us would grasp the profound gravity of the legacy we hoped to leave behind.

In one chamber, we stumbled upon a room aglow with the ethereal light of countless lanterns. They floated, suspended mid-air, their flames flickering with stories yet untold. Here, the boundary between the temporal and the eternal seemed perilously thin, as though one could reach out and pluck moments from both past and future.

It was the Library of Legacies—a place where the journeys of countless souls were inscribed, from the most illustrious to the most obscure. Each lantern held a volume, a chronicle of someone's essence, their trials, triumphs, and tribulations.

In reverent silence, Clarissa approached a lantern, its flame casting a dancing reflection that mirrored her own eyes. As she opened its volume, her fingers trembled. "It's my great-grandmother," she murmured, the weight of her lineage apparent in her gaze. "A woman of resilience and grace, whose legacy was etched not in grandiose acts, but in the compassionate whispers she left in her wake."

Adolwolf, curious, reached for a tome from a lantern that pulsed with a golden hue. "It's an ancestor of mine—a philosopher. His ideas were deemed radical in his era, but they paved the way for generations of thinkers. His legacy was his vision, one that transcended the confines of his own time."

Drawn to a lantern with an ember-red glow, I too found a chronicle, the pages recounting tales of my forebears—artisans and adventurers, dreamers and doers. Each narrative was a reminder that legacies weren't just the summation of our actions but also the intangible impressions we left behind.

In the midst of these discoveries, the very fabric of Ashcroft seemed to pulse with a newfound vibrancy. We began to perceive a conundrum—the mansion itself, while an embodiment of countless legacies, yearned for its own story to be remembered. Its walls hungered to be more than mere spectators; they sought to be catalysts, guiding souls towards their destinies and ensuring their legacies wouldn't be buried beneath the sands of time.

Beyond the Library of Legacies, the corridors unfurled like the tentacles of some ancient creature, leading us deeper into the mansion's enigmatic embrace. Flickering candlelight danced on the walls, casting shadows that seemed to shimmer with the vestiges of days long gone.

It was in one such dimly lit corridor that we happened upon a vast, ornate door, its wooden surface adorned with intricate carvings of intertwined vines and two headed creatures of an amphibian nature. As if guided by some unseen force, Clarissa extended her hand and turned the crystalline doorknob. The door moved silently open to reveal the Conservatory of Chronos.

The main entrance was a grand archway, etched with runes that constantly shifted and moved, representing the fluidity of time. Stepping inside, we were met with an expansive, open-roofed chamber, the walls of which were lined with tiers of intricate clockwork mechanisms, every gear and cog in perpetual motion. Time, here, we soon realized, is not linear. It ebbs and flows, sways, and dances, often in response to those who visit.

Its structures were tall, slender spires that reached skywards, mirroring the helix of a DNA strand. Each spire was crafted from an iridescent material, unknown to the realms of human science, that glimmered with a pearlescent sheen, casting ethereal rainbows under the sunlight.

In stark contrast to the muted ambiance of the previous rooms, this chamber radiated a luminescent splendor. Its vast expanse was dominated by an immense hourglass, its sands flowing in mesmerizing patterns, as if time itself was being woven and rewoven. The sands within never diminished nor fully accumulated on either side; they are in an eternal, mesmerizing loop of flow. But this is no ordinary hourglass. It's said that the sands themselves are fragments of epochs gone by, every grain a moment, a memory, a world of its own. Around the hourglass stood statues of men and women, their expressions etched with determination and contemplation.

"These," Adolwolf murmured, his voice imbued with a reverence, "are the Custodians of Time. Each represents an individual who profoundly altered the course of history, not by their stature in society, but by the depth of their conviction."

Gazing upon those statues, it became evident that legacy was not merely about remembrance but resonance. It was about setting forth actions that would continue to shape the world long after one's ephemeral existence had faded.

However, the true marvel of the conservatory wasn't merely its statues or even the grand hourglass; it was the photonic waltz of motes of light. They elegantly danced around us, each a fragment of a moment, a memory, a choice. The Photonic Waltz of Light is a phenomenon that graces the Conservatory during the equinoxes. As the sun aligns perfectly overhead, a spectacle unfolds. The iridescent spires channel sunlight into prismatic beams that dance through the conservatory. But this is no mere play of sunlight. It is a choreographed ballad.

These beams of light weren't just radiant; they were alive. They moved in synchronicity, swirling, twirling, creating intricate patterns in the air. Sometimes two beams merged into a luminescent embrace, producing colors previously unseen by human eyes. As they danced, they sung - a soothing tune that whispers tales from bygone eras, of civilizations lost, of heroes forgotten.

It's as if, for a brief moment, we had become intertwined with the very fabric of time. Memories not our own flooded our minds: a laughing child from a century past, a lover's embrace on a forgotten shoreline, a battle cry on an alien world.

The waltz lasted for what felt like both an eternity and a mere second. And as the final beams retreated, plunging the Conservatory into a peaceful dimness, we were left with a new understanding of time's vastness and the interconnectedness of all moments, past, present, and future.

"The essence of our legacies," Clarissa whispered, her eyes alight with realization, "isn't in the span of our lives but in the depth of our moments."

A mote settled on my palm, illuminating a distant memory of my youth—a simple act of kindness, a shared laugh, a silent tear. It was a stark reminder that the threads of our legacy are woven not just from monumental feats but from everyday gestures, often overlooked yet profoundly impactful.

The conservatory was a sanctum of understanding. Within its luminous walls, we began to fathom that while Ashcroft was a vessel of the past, it was also a beacon for the future. Its mysteries were not puzzles to be solved but lessons to be absorbed, guiding each visitor to recognize their potential impact upon the tapestry of existence.

And as the sands of the great hourglass flowed, we were left to ponder: What legacy would we wish to create? What moments would we craft? And how might we, in our fleeting time, leave an indelible mark upon the vast expanse of history?

Chapter 2: A Maze Of Light And Shadow

Beyond the walls of the Conservatory of Chronos, the enigmatic embrace of Ashcroft intensified. The mansion's architecture evolved, hinting at epochs and eras long buried beneath the weight of millennia. Here, cobblestone blended seamlessly with burnished metal, ancient wood intertwined with gleaming crystal. It was as if Ashcroft was an eternal entity, evolving and devolving, forever in flux yet staunchly timeless.

As we delved deeper, the hallways unraveled like a serpentine puzzle, leading us into the Labyrinth of Luminescence. Here, the dim corridors were replaced by a maze bathed in iridescent light, where every twist and turn shimmered with spectral hues.

"Legend speaks of this place," Adolwolf murmured, his voice a blend of awe and trepidation. "It's said that the Labyrinth is the very heart of Ashcroft, where one's legacy is not just observed but truly lived." With every step, the very atmosphere pulsated with palpable memories. Clarissa, wandering a few paces ahead, stumbled into an alcove that transported her into a fleeting scene from her ancestral past—a bustling marketplace where her great-grandmother, with youthful exuberance, haggled spiritedly, her laughter echoing through time.

Meanwhile, I was drawn towards a vortex of soft amber light. Stepping into it, I found myself on a rugged coastline, watching a distant ancestor, an artisan, painstakingly sculpt a masterpiece from a once nondescript piece of driftwood. The passion, the commitment, and the vision were all within grasp, painting a vivid picture of the legacy he left through his art.

But the Labyrinth was not merely a conduit to the past. As we ventured further, we began to encounter future potentialities, visions of what could be—a testament to Ashcroft's intricate interweaving of time's fabric.

In one luminescent passage, Adolwolf saw himself in an academic hall, passionately debating with future scholars, his ideas forming the cornerstone of new philosophical movements. It was a glimpse into a potential legacy, one where his thoughts and musings might shape minds for generations to come.

"The Labyrinth," Clarissa whispered, her voice peppered with emotion, "doesn't just show us where we come from but where we might lead."

Indeed, the maze was more than just a repository of memories and possibilities; it was a mirror, reflecting the profound impact each soul might imprint upon history. The Labyrinth of Luminescence challenged each visitor to not just observe but to introspect, to reconcile with one's past, and to envision a legacy that could illuminate the future.

Navigating the serpentine intricacies of the Labyrinth, a new sensation began to envelop us—a weighty realization that legacy, in its essence, transcends linear chronology. It's not merely about past deeds or future potentialities but about the very present moment, where choices are made, paths are forged, and ripples are initiated.

I was ensnared by an azure luminescence that led to a mirrored chamber. The reflections weren't of the present but a myriad of potential futures. In one, I saw myself as a mentor, guiding young minds, imparting wisdom distilled from experiences. In another, I was an explorer, charting unknown terrains, leaving behind tales of courage and discovery. The chamber, in its silent eloquence, posed a challenge: Which reflection would I wish to crystallize into reality?

Meanwhile, Clarissa found herself amidst a cascade of emerald light, which unveiled her as a matriarch, weaving tales for her grandchildren, passing on wisdom and nurturing a lineage where each generation grew stronger, kinder, and more resilient.

Adolwolf's journey led him to a corridor bathed in golden luminescence, where scrolls floated mid-air, each inscribed with profound philosophical musings, some ancient, some yet to be written. Among them, he found his own thoughts, not just those he had already formulated but also those that lay dormant, waiting to be awakened. "This Labyrinth," he mused, the profundity of the moment evident in his voice, "isn't just about the legacy we leave for the world. It's equally about the legacy we craft for ourselves, the narrative we create, refine, and embrace throughout our lives."

As we reconvened within the labyrinth, the collected energy of the photon bathed mazed seemed to intensify, as if responding to our shared revelations. The luminescent hues began to merge, creating a kaleidoscope of colors, each representing the greatest of legacies, intertwining, and resonating in harmonious synchrony.

Suddenly, from the confluence of lights emerged an ethereal figure, a guardian of sorts, her countenance reflecting both ageless wisdom and youthful exuberance. "I am Lyria, the Keeper of Legacies," she intoned, her voice a melodic blend of eons gone by and epochs yet to dawn. "You've traversed the memories and potentialities, but the true test of legacy lies ahead. For it's not just about understanding its depth but also about making the conscious choice to shape, nurture, and perpetuate it."

With a beckoning gesture, she led the way, her form shimmering with every step—promising deeper introspection, more profound revelations, and an understanding of the timeless tapestry that binds us all.

Chapter 3: The Echoes of Elysium

Dawn's tendrils had begun to creep through the ornate windows of Ashcroft, casting diaphanous shadows that melded seamlessly with the mansion's mysterious nature. Having emerged from the labyrinthine depths, the ethereal landscape of the mansion's grounds unfolded before us, revealing gardens that seemed to straddle both reality and reverie.

The flora here wasn't typical—trees with silvered leaves whispered ancient tales, flowers with luminescent petals danced to the song of the zephyr, and crystalline brooks murmured riddles of days yet unborn. This was the Echoes of Elysium, a sanctum where nature itself bore testament to legacies left behind.

Guided by the ever-elusive Lyria, we meandered through the gardens, each step revealing nature's tribute to souls that had, in their own unique ways, enriched the world. A cobalt bloom unveiled the tale of a poet whose verses had mended broken hearts. A gnarled tree, its branches reaching skyward, resonated with the tenacity of an explorer who'd charted unexplored terrains.

Clarissa, her senses ever attuned to the arcane, was the first to spot the Circle of Chronicles—a secluded glade wherein stood stone plinths, each etched with symbols and sigils. "These," Lyria elucidated, her fingers delicately tracing a symbol, "are the epitomes of legacies. Each represents a soul, an ethos, a contribution to the cosmos."

Adolwolf, inquisitive, approached a plinth bearing the symbol of an open tome. As he touched it, the symbol glowed, unveiling the narrative of a scholar who'd bridged cultures, teaching tolerance and understanding in divisive times. The stone didn't just recount the tale; it evoked the very essence, the emotions, the challenges, and the triumphs.

As I wandered, a particular plinth, adorned with an intricate compass, beckoned. Upon touch, it unfurled the odyssey of an ancestor, a navigator, who, guided by the stars, had united distant shores, bringing tales from afar to eager listeners at home.

Yet, the true marvel of the Echoes of Elysium was its affirmation that every legacy, grand or subtle, echoed in eternity. It was a confirmation of the belief that while bodies may perish, ideals and influences persist, perpetually shaping the world.

As the first light of dawn kissed the horizon, we, guided by the spectral wisdom of Lyria, stood poised at the cusp of deeper revelations, eager to unravel the many ways in which legacies intertwined, influenced, and immortalized themselves in the halls of time.

Amidst the glimmering flora and otherworldly plinths, a peculiar resonance emanated, a meticulous harmony that seemed to beckon us further into the heart of Elysium. Following the siren call, we discovered its source—a serene pool, its waters so limpid that it mirrored not just our reflections but also the very souls we harbored.

Known as the Reflections of Resonance, this sacred reservoir held the distilled memories of countless legacies, each ripple representing an act, a decision, a moment that had shifted the course of history.

Clarissa knelt by the pool's edge, and as her fingertips grazed its surface, visions cascaded forth. Scenes of her lineage—an ancestor standing resilient against a tempest, ensuring the safety of his community; a foremother teaching her daughters the art of herbal healing, preserving age-old traditions while instilling innovation.

Adolwolf, with a hesitancy borne of reverence, touched the waters and was immediately ensnared by a tableau of thinkers and philosophers, debating, pondering, and forever questing for enlightenment. His lineage was one of thought, of challenging norms, of perpetually seeking understanding amidst the chaos of existence.

As I approached, the pool seemed to pulse, recognizing a familiar essence. Tentatively, I reached out, and the waters responded, unveiling a mosaic of moments—some from the distant past, others from a conceivable future. There was an architect, building bridges both literal and metaphorical; a storyteller weaving narratives that soothed souls and ignited imaginations; a guardian standing sentinel over ancient woods, ensuring nature's voice was always heard.

Lyria, watching us from the periphery, whispered, "The pool doesn't merely show what was or what might be. It reveals the interconnectedness of legacies—the way a single act can reverberate through time, impacting countless souls in unlimited ways."

As the sun ascended, casting prismatic hues upon Elysium, a profound epiphany dawned. Legacy wasn't just about monumental deeds or renowned accomplishments. It was crafted from the myriad minute moments, the seemingly inconsequential choices, the silent sacrifices, and the whispered words of wisdom.

The Echoes of Elysium served not just as a window to the past but as a clarion call for the future—a reminder that every soul, no matter how fleeting its existence, had the potential to leave an indelible mark, to create waves that would resonate through the corridors of time.

Beyond the mesmeric pool, the Echoes of Elysium unfurled into a vast orchard, its trees laden with ethereal fruits, each shimmering and pulsating with life. This was the Orchard of Offerings, where the tangible manifestations of legacies bore fruit, quite literally.

Lyria, leading us with her characteristic elegance, proclaimed "Each tree here was born from a seed of intention, nurtured by deeds, and now bears the fruits of legacy. To partake is to comprehend the very essence of a legacy's influence."

Clarissa, her curiosity piqued, reached for a fruit that gleamed like burnished gold. Upon consumption, she was enveloped in a profound serenity. Visions of a great healer in her lineage, whose hands and herbs had mended both body and soul, overwhelmed her. The fruit imparted not just the knowledge but the very emotions, the trials, tribulations, and triumphs of that healer's journey.

Adolwolf, always methodical in his approach, studied the trees before selecting a sapphire-hued fruit. As he bit into it, his demeanor transformed—his eyes widened with wonderment, his posture reflecting newfound wisdom. He saw, felt, and lived the days of a philosopher-ancestor who'd questioned, contemplated, and eventually scribed doctrines that brought solace to many during tumultuous times.

I, unsurprisingly, was inexplicably drawn to a tree with opalescent fruits, each exuding an enigmatic luminescence. Hesitant, yet compelled, I took a bite. A maelstrom of emotions engulfed me. Visions of champion defenders, each contributing to the tapestry of time in their own unique ways, played before my eyes. There was love, loss, valor, and vulnerability—a whirlwind of human experience.

"The Orchard," Lyria elucidated with a gaze that spanned eternities, "offers a rare gift—the ability to truly internalize the essence of legacies. To partake is to understand that each legacy, regardless of its magnitude, contributes to the grand mosaic of existence."

As we continued our journey, the very air of Elysium seemed imbued with whispered tales, each breeze carrying anecdotes of valor, each ray of sunlight illuminating stories of hope. But it was the underlying message that resonated most deeply—that every soul, through acts of love, courage, kindness, and wisdom, had the power to shape not just their destiny but the destiny of epochs yet to dawn.

But the day, with its revelations and resonances, began to wane. With the Echoes of Elysium singing in our hearts, we set forth, eager to delve deeper, to understand more profoundly the enigma of legacy and the role each of us plays in this ageless narrative.

As we, now deeply entwined with the chronicles of our ancestry, ventured forth, we stumbled upon a clearing where time itself seemed to pause—a celestial amphitheater, the Theater of Thoughts, where the very air quivered with anticipation. Seated on its gossamer tiers were phantasmal figures, the stewards of legacies long past, watching enactments of memories, aspirations, and moments of profound epiphanies. These were not mere recreations, but living resonances of times bygone, brought to life through the sheer force of collective memory and intention.

Lyria beckoned, her voice redolent with nostalgia and reverence. "This theater is where legacies are celebrated and remembered. Here, past, present, and future confluence, allowing souls to relive, reflect upon, and revel in the infinite tapestries they've woven."

And at that very moment a performance began to commence. The ethereal figures hushed, their attention converging on the central stage where a soft, radiant glow began to form. From it emerged two spectral dancers, their forms weaving a tale of love, sacrifice, and resilience. It was a story from Clarissa's lineage—of two lovers separated by war, yet whose love transcended boundaries and time, leaving an indomitable mark on generations to come.

Moved to tears, Clarissa whispered, "Their love story has been told in my family for generations. But witnessing it here, feeling its very essence... it's overwhelming."

As the tale reached its poignant climax, another began. This was from Adolwolf's heritage—a tale of a philosopher who, against the backdrop of societal upheaval, sowed the seeds of enlightenment, challenging dogmas, and sparking revolutions of thought. I watched, enraptured, waiting for a vision from my lineage. And then it began—an evocative portrayal of an artist, my great-grandmother, capturing life's fleeting moments on her canvas, immortalizing them for posterity. Her art wasn't just a personal legacy, but a cultural treasure, reminding future generations of the beauty and fragility of existence.

The performances, though varied in their themes, converged on a singular truth—that the legacy one leaves behind isn't just about grand deeds or monumental achievements. It's about the lives touched, the hearts moved, and the souls illuminated.

As the Theater of Thoughts dimmed, signaling the end of the performances, the weight and wonder of the day pressed upon us. Elysium had unveiled the mosaic of legacies in all its intricacy, reminding us of our place in the grand creation of existence.

Lyria, with a smile that bridged ages, whispered, "Remember, every echo, every resonance, every memory you've witnessed here began as a mere whisper, a single choice. The legacy you wish to weave is in your hands."

With hearts brimming with newfound wisdom and souls ignited with purpose, we prepared to leave the theater, ready to embrace our roles as the next custodians of legacy in the enigmatic realm of Ashcroft.

The departure from the Theater of Thoughts was accompanied by an overwhelming sensation of having traveled through centuries, even as mere hours had elapsed. The verdant pathways of Elysium seemed now to sway with deeper reverence, as if acknowledging our intimate communion with the legacies that had walked these very grounds.

Suddenly, the ethereal atmosphere grew taut with an electric charge. Whispering winds carried fragments of melodies and murmurs that felt oddly familiar, and yet, profoundly enigmatic. We found ourselves drawn to the Confluence Cauldron, a place where individual legacies merged, creating a collective consciousness—a repository of shared wisdom, aspirations, and the truly unique spirit of humanity.

It was said that to truly understand one's legacy, one must first grasp the intertwined destinies of countless souls, observing how individual threads of existence weave into the grand tapestry of the universe.

Lyria, with her eyes reflecting galaxies of experiences, intoned, "This cauldron is the culmination of Elysium's lessons. Here, singular legacies intertwine, reminding us that while each journey is unique, they are all interdependent, contributing to the macro-cosmic narrative of existence."

The cauldron, shimmering with iridescent hues, beckoned us closer. Within its depths, visions stirred—of shared joys and sorrows, of communities coming together in times of adversity, of the countless intersections of fate that had brought about monumental shifts in the course of history.

Adolwolf, his analytical mind always probing, reflected aloud, "It's a humbling realization. While our individual legacies are significant, it's the confluence of our actions, choices, and intentions with those of others that shapes the world." Clarissa, her spirit visibly uplifted, added, "It's like a cosmic dance, isn't it? Each of us contributing our unique steps, yet all moving in harmony to the rhythm of existence." As I peered into the cauldron, a revelation dawned. My legacy, our legacies, were not isolated chronicles. They were part of an intricate, interwoven story—a narrative of hope, resilience, love, and transformation.

As the dusk began its gentle descent upon Elysium, casting long shadows and bathing everything in a golden embrace, the three of us—our souls forever changed—sat by the Confluence Cauldron, reflecting on our journey. Lyria, her voice soft as a lullaby, whispered the essence of our pilgrimage, "Elysium has many lessons, but its core message is simple: To leave a legacy is human, but to understand and honor the interconnectedness of those legacies is divine."

The day's revelations, the mysteries unraveled, and the wisdom imparted coalesced into a singular resolve. We were not mere spectators in the theater of life. We were its playwrights, its actors, its custodians—each with the power to leave an indelible mark in this great universe of boundless time.

Chapter 4: Endless Alcove

Morning broke over Ashcroft with a quiet reverence. The luminescent rays of dawn painted the horizon with hues of hope, hinting at the revelations yet to come. Elysium, though familiar in its beauty, seemed to emanate a new allure—a magnetic pull towards deeper truths and concealed corridors of comprehension. The first hours were spent in reflective solitude, each of us absorbing the lessons, reminiscences, and realizations of the previous day. The Echoes of Elysium still resonated deeply within our souls, underscoring the significance of interconnected destinies.

A sudden gust, laden with the scents of ancient papyrus and time-worn leather, beckoned us towards the Archive Alcove, a repository of chronicles and memoirs. It was whispered that within its walls, one could decipher not just personal legacies but the very undercurrents of history that propelled them. The Alcove, an architectural marvel, towered ahead. Its entrance was flanked by statues of Guardians of Gravitas, beings believed to hold the collective wisdom of ages. Their marble eyes, while stoic, seemed to shimmer with the secrets they safeguarded.

Lyria, her steps echoing with purpose, announced, "To truly fathom the depth of a legacy, one must also understand its context—the era, the ethos, and the events that shaped it."

As we ventured deeper into the Alcove, the atmosphere grew denser with the weight of millennia. Thousands times thousands of scrolls, books, and ghostly recordings surrounded us, each bearing witness to the lives, decisions, and dreams of those who walked before us.

Clarissa, with a glint of intrigue, unrolled a scroll that depicted the era of great maritime explorers. Their voyages, driven by curiosity and courage, not only expanded geographical boundaries but also the horizons of human understanding. Adolwolf, however, was engrossed in an ethereal tome that detailed the Renaissance—a period of unparalleled artistic and intellectual resurgence. The luminaries of that era, through their creations and contemplation, had left legacies that still illuminated the corridors of modern thought. Drawn to a peculiar orb, I hesitated before touching it. The moment I did, visions of ancestral storytellers flooded my senses—their tales, while simple, held profound truths about love, sacrifice, and resilience.

Within the Archive Alcove, it became evident that legacies were not birthed in isolation. They were shaped, molded, and influenced by the zeitgeist of their times. Understanding this context was pivotal in appreciating the true magnitude and reach of one's legacy. As we navigated this vast compendium of history, the lines between past, present, and future began to blur, reminding us of the timeless nature of legacies and their undying impact on the ever-evolving narrative of humanity.

As we stood among the towering shelves and endless halls, the air was redolent with whispered tales from epochs long gone. These were more than mere records; they breathed with life, carrying the very essence of the souls whose stories they enshrined.

Lyria, a beacon of wisdom, explained, "The Alcove is not just a repository, but a living testament. It echoes with the dreams, desires, and determinations of those who dared to leave their mark."

Clarissa, having moved from the scrolls, now hovered over an ancient-looking map, the continents depicted upon it still unfamiliar, yet hinting at lands and civilizations yet to be discovered. "Look," she murmured, tracing a path with her finger, "The journeys charted here are not merely of land and sea, but also of the heart and soul. These explorers, in their quest for the unknown, unraveled deeper truths about themselves and the world."

Adolwolf, always introspective, looked up from a manuscript penned by thinkers of antiquity. "It's enlightening," he mentioned, "how thoughts and ideas, when given voice and nurtured, can shape eras and craft legacies that reverberate through centuries."

As for me, I was drawn to a gilded mirror, seemingly out of place amidst the chronicles. Yet, as I approached, the mirror's surface rippled, unveiling scenes from my lineage—each reflection showcasing a forebearer, their choices, challenges, and the legacies they had bequeathed to subsequent generations.

One reflection, in particular, arrested my attention. An ancestor, a visionary sculptor, chiseling away with fervent dedication, not just to create art, but to convey eternal truths. Through his art, he revealed the multi facets of human emotion and existence. Lyria, sensing my profound connection, whispered, "Every legacy is a mosaic, assembled piece by piece, choice by choice. This mirror reflects not just the grand moments, but also the seemingly inconsequential decisions that, in their entirety, shape destinies."

The Archive Alcove, with its boundless wisdom and insights, impressed upon us the profound realization that each individual, regardless of era or circumstance, possesses the power to sculpt their legacy. The choices made, the paths taken, and the passions pursued, all converge to create a unified force of care that transcends temporal confines.

And as twilight's soft embrace began to blanket Ashcroft, we departed the Alcove, our spirits buoyed with newfound understanding. The journey through Elysium was shaping up to be more than a mere exploration—it was becoming a transformative odyssey, awakening us to the monumental potential within, to leave legacies that echo through eternity.

With every step away from the Alcove, the evening air grew crisp, and the silhouettes of the ancient structures of Ashcroft stood in stark contrast against the deepening twilight. The sky was painted with strokes of lavender and gold, heralding the mysteries of the impending night.

Elysium, in its nocturnal splendor, revealed a different face—a canvas of constellations, each star a legacy in its own right, silently narrating tales of cosmic endeavors. We found ourselves at the Observatory of Origins, a place where the stories of the stars intertwined with the tales of humankind.

Clarissa, forever enchanted by the cosmos, exclaimed, "Each star, much like each soul, has its own narrative, its own radiant legacy. Their light, even after eons, continues to guide, inspire, and remind us of the vastness of the universe and our role within it."

Adolwolf, his eyes reflecting the endless expanse above, pondered aloud, "The constellations, age-old formations, have guided sailors, inspired poets, and offered solace to lonely souls. In their silent brilliance, they've shaped countless destinies on Earth."

Lyria, her gaze fixed upon the Polaris, the unwavering North Star, mused, "Just as the stars have their destined place in the firmament, so do we in the grand tapestry of life. Our choices, much like the burning cores of these celestial bodies, radiate outwards, influencing paths and shaping futures in ways we might never fully fathom."

I, lost in the symphony of stars, felt a profound connection with my ancestors, whose eyes had once marveled at the same celestial wonders. In that fleeting moment, time seemed to collapse, binding past, present, and future in an eternal dance.

Amidst the profound silences and whispered revelations, a soft melody wafted through the Observatory. An ancient lullaby of Elysium, it spoke of the legacies left behind, of the impermanence of existence, and the eternal nature of the legacies we leave behind. The lyrics, while in an ancient dialect, resonated deeply, reinforcing the universal truths of life, love, and legacy. As the night deepened, we reclined on the cool marble of the Observatory, letting the wisdom of the cosmos wash over us. The countless legacies, both terrestrial and celestial, reinforced our purpose and resolve.

As the moon ascended her throne in the celestial expanse, a soft, calming mist began to envelop Elysium. From the Observatory's vantage, we observed streams of this ethereal fog winding through the Ashcroft Mansion, enveloping structures and statues, rendering them dreamlike and mystical.

Lyria, her eyes alight with anticipation, said, "Tonight, Elysium unveils one of its most arcane and profound realms—the Dimension of Dreams. In it lie the worlds crafted by dreamers, visionaries, and seers through millennia. Each dream is a legacy, a world in itself, waiting to be explored."

Clarissa, her curiosity palpable, questioned, "But how does one navigate such a dimension, where the boundaries of reality are blurred, and the realms of imagination reign supreme?"

Adolwolf, having come across references in his earlier readings, elucidated, "Dreams are constructed from our deepest desires, fears, and aspirations. By attuning to these, one can traverse this dimension, experiencing worlds both wondrous and bewildering."

As Lryia finished speaking, a great shaking was felt as we were lifted into the air and descended from the Observatory, drawn irresistibly towards the heart of the mist. As we ventured deeper, the very fabric of reality began to warp. Distinct landscapes, born from the dreams of countless souls, converged and melded, creating a mesmerizing collection of sights, sounds, and sensations.

In one moment, we stood atop majestic mountains, carved from crystalline hopes, their peaks touching the heavens. In the next, we wandered through labyrinthine forests, where the trees whispered secrets from ages past, their leaves shimmering with forgotten memories.

I found myself in a city constructed entirely of melodies—each structure a symphony, each alleyway a lilting tune. The denizens, ephemeral entities of harmony, sang of their creators' aspirations, of love unrequited, of victories celebrated, and of legacies yearned for.

Lyria, in her majestic role as our guide, reminded us, "Remember, in the Dimension of Dreams, the realms are transient, shaped and reshaped by the collective consciousness of dreamers. But within each dreamscape lies a kernel of truth, a legacy waiting to be deciphered."

As dawn's first light threatened, we began our retreat from this enigmatic dimension, our souls enriched by the many dreams we had traversed. The dreams, though intangible, held weight, each a seed of the dreamer's essence and the legacy they wished to leave behind.

Emerging from the mist, Elysium's reality greeted us once more, but now imbued with a deeper understanding. Dreams, we realized, were not just fleeting fantasies but powerful legacies, capable of crafting worlds and influencing generations to come. In that sanctum of sleep, within each human beings theater of the mind, we all held the power to leave an indelible mark, an everlasting legacy in the worlds we conjured.

Chapter 5: The Dreamers Descent

As Elysium's dawn cast golden beams upon the ancient city, the four of us congregated at a serene plaza, our minds still awash with the fantastical dreamscapes we had traversed. However, as with all moments of tranquility in Ashcroft, this was soon to be disrupted. A figure, enshrouded in robes of midnight blue and embroidered with galaxies, stepped forth from the shadows of a forgotten monument. The very air seemed to grow cold, yet paradoxically alive, with a latent energy.

"Welcome, travelers of time and legacy," the figure intoned, his voice echoing with ageless wisdom. "I am Morphean, Guardian of Dreams. While your journey through the dream realm was sanctioned, there are truths you've uncovered that were meant to remain veiled. " Lyria, always poised, responded, "Morphean, we meant no transgression. Our quest is to understand legacy, both seen and unseen. The world of dreams offers insights profound and transformative."

Morphean's eyes, deep pools of cosmic knowledge, fixed upon me.

"You," he began, his voice taking on a smoother quality, "bear a legacy unlike any other. In your dreams lies a world that has the potential to alter the very fabric of Elysium."

Stunned, I tried to comprehend his revelation. My dreams? A significant legacy?

Clarissa, sensing my disquiet, interjected, "What do you mean? What has been seen in our companion's dreams?"

The Guardian hesitated, then finally divulged, "Every dream adds to Elysium's tapestry, but some dreams possess a potency that can shape reality itself. In Rhinehearts dreams lies a world teetering on the brink of genesis, a world that can either elevate Elysium to unparalleled heights or plunge it into chaos."

Adolwolf, sense alerted, responded, "You speak of the ancient prophecies, of a Dreamer whose visions hold the key to Elysium's destiny."

Morphean nodded, "Indeed. The Dreamer was foretold to wander into Elysium, and with them, they'd bring a dream that carries the weight of worlds. Whether this weight would be a boon or bane remains to be seen."

I, overwhelmed, finally found my voice, "But why me? And how do we ensure this dream shapes a legacy of hope and not destruction?"

The enigmatic Guardian, drawing a silver vial from his robe, answered, "Within this vial is the Elixir of Lucidity. It will allow you to enter your dream consciously and navigate its intricacies. Your companions will accompany you, guiding and aiding in ensuring the dream's legacy is one of harmony."

As Morphean handed me the vial, the weight of responsibility felt tangible.

In the heart of Ashcroft, a secluded courtyard known to few as the Garden of Reverie lay nestled between structures of timeless splendor. It was here, amidst blossoming moonflowers and luminescent vines, that our expedition into the dreamscape was to commence.

Morphean, having guided us to this serene enclave, began preparations. A circular formation of intricate runes, radiating an ethereal glow, was etched upon the ground. "This," he declared, "is the Nexus of Dreams. It will ensure your passage into the dream remains tethered to Elysium's reality."

Lyria, her eyes reflecting the runes' luminescence, inquired, "Once inside the dream, what are we to expect?"

Morphean, pausing to infuse the formation with an essence unknown, responded, "Dreams, especially ones of potent legacy, are reflections of one's innermost self. They are realms of symbolism, emotion, and raw essence. You may encounter challenges, but they are manifestations of inner conflicts and desires. Resolve them, and the dream will stabilize."

Adolwolf, eyes alight with curiosity, asked, "But if this dream bears the potential to reshape Elysium, wouldn't its challenges be monumental?"

The Guardian, his gaze heavy with the gravity of millennia, said, "Indeed. The challenges will be monumental, for the dream's legacy mirrors the magnitude of its potential impact."

With feelings of haste, I uncapped the vial containing the Elixir of Lucidity. The liquid shimmered with a brilliance akin to stardust. As I consumed it, a gentle warmth spread through me, and the world around began to blur, giving way to the realm of dreams.

Clarissa, Lyria, and Adolwolf, after partaking in the Elixir, joined me as we stepped into the Nexus of Dreams. A vortex of colors and sensations enveloped us, and in mere moments, we found ourselves in a landscape simultaneously familiar yet alien.

Endless meadows stretched before us, their grasses iridescent and ever-shifting. A horizon marked by floating islands, cascading waterfalls that defied gravity, and skies painted with colors beyond mortal comprehension beckoned us forward.

Yet, amidst this beauty lay dissonance. Cracks of foreboding darkness marred the landscape, and ominous storm clouds loomed, threatening to unleash their fury. It was clear that the dream, while resplendent, was on the brink of chaos.

"We must navigate this realm," I asserted, "and mend the fractures. Only then can we ensure the dream's legacy is one of hope."

As our journey began, the first challenge soon manifested—a vast chasm, its depths an abyss of oblivion. The only means of traversal was a bridge, constructed from fragmented memories, each piece representing moments of joy, sorrow, love, and loss.

And as we set forth on this perilous path, guided by the luminescence of dreams and the weight of legacy, we were reminded of the fragile yet formidable nature of existence, and the spirit required to shape one's destiny.

Each fragment of the bridge flashed with memories. With every step, fleeting moments sprang to life, some touching the soul with warmth and others searing it with regret. Navigating the bridge wasn't just about physical traversal but emotional reconciliation.

Clarissa, empathy abound, paused at a fragment which radiated a deep blue hue. "This memory," she murmured, her voice laden with emotion, "is one of profound sadness, yet there's an undertone of hope. It's a reminder that even in our deepest despairs, a spark of hope can ignite transformation."

Adolwolf, whose analytical mind often saw beyond the evident, mused at another fragment glowing a vibrant gold. "This one speaks of achievement. But not the kind that comes from personal accolades. It's a shared victory, a testament to unity and collaboration."

Lyria, her fingers brushing a fragment exuding a serene green, whispered, "A moment of tranquility, a respite within chaos. Such moments, though ghostly, anchor our souls, providing strength to face oncoming tempests."

And I, drawn to a fragment radiating an intense crimson, felt my heart race. "This is passion," I breathed, "a fierce desire to change, to make a difference, to leave an indelible mark."

However, as we neared the bridge's end, the fragments grew darker, muddied with doubt and insecurity. The bridge trembled, and from the abyss below, shadows began to reach out, attempting to drag the memories—and us—into oblivion.

Lyria, her voice unwavering, declared, "These are the fears and uncertainties that plague every soul. To conquer them is to solidify the dream's foundation."

With determination, we each confronted these darkened memories, infusing them with our collective strengths, experiences, and convictions. The shadows receded, and as the final fragment was cleansed, the bridge solidified, leading us safely to the other side of the chasm. Beyond us in the near distance we perceived a welcoming meadow.

Upon reaching the meadow, we were greeted by a magnificent tree, its branches touching the skies and roots delving deep into the earth. The Tree of Dreams, as Morphean had once recounted to story tellers who once told tales of old.

But around it swirled a maelstrom, memories caught in a whirlwind of confusion, threatening to uproot the tree.

"We must stabilize the dream at its very core," I asserted. "This tree, it's the heart of it all."

As we approached, memories—both luminous and shadowed—hurled towards us, demanding resolution. Together, we navigated the storm, understanding that to ensure a legacy of hope, one must confront both the light and the shadows of one's existence.

With each memory confronted and reconciled, the tempest began to wane. The skies cleared, revealing the brilliance of the dream realm in its full glory.

Yet, as tranquility settled, an echoing voice resonated through the realm. "Your endeavors here, noble as they might be, have only just commenced. The dream's legacy, while now stable, is yet to be fully realized."

We turned to see a familiar figure emerging from the tree's vast trunk - Morphean, the Guardian of Dreams.

"Our journey in the dreamscape continues," he pronounced. "For in dreams lie not just memories of the past, but visions of the future."

The once tumultuous landscape now radiated serenity, but the enigmatic expression on Morphean's face suggested the journey's pinnacle had yet to be reached. Drawing closer to the magnificent Tree of Dreams, we noticed its bark was inscribed with countless runes, each glowing faintly and resonating with whispered echoes from time long past.

"The Tree is not just a beacon within the dream," Morphean began, his voice mirroring the gentle rustle of the tree's leaves. "It's a chronicle, an archive of legacies past and visions of futures potential. Each rune, each etching is a dreamer's hope, fear, or aspiration. To truly influence Elysium's future, you must etch your own legacy upon this ancient bark."

Adolwolf, curiosity realized, arched an eyebrow, "You mean to literally inscribe upon the tree?"

Morphean nodded, "But not with tools of the material world. Your intent, your hope, your very essence will leave its mark."

Lyria approached a vacant space on the tree's sprawling surface, her fingers barely grazing its ancient bark. Closing her eyes, she delved deep into her essence, her aspirations for a harmonious future, her dreams of unity amongst Elysium's denizens. As her spirit communed with the Tree, a luminous rune materialized—depicting two hands clasped in unity.

Clarissa, inspired by Lyria's actions, soon followed. Her dreams for Elysium were rooted in empathy, understanding, and the acceptance of all narratives. As she concentrated, a rune took form—a heart intertwined with an open book.

Adolwolf approached hesitantly. Though often guarded, his dreams for Elysium were profound. He yearned for knowledge to be freely available, for innovation to be encouraged. His rune emerged as an illuminated lantern, casting away the shadows of ignorance.

It was then my turn. I approached the tree, thoughts swirling. What did I truly desire for Elysium? I thought of the adventures, the revelations, the importance of legacies, and our journey within the dreamscape. I dreamt of a world where every individual recognized the power of their legacy, understanding that even in the ethereal realm of dreams, tangible change could be wrought. My rune appeared—a spiral, representing the continuous journey of life, with a star at its center, symbolizing the guiding light of legacy.

With our runes etched upon the Tree of Dreams, Morphean declared, "Elysium's dreamscape has been stabilized, but the ultimate journey commences when you awaken. The challenges you've faced here, the legacies you've chosen to etch, they must guide your actions in the waking world."

Suddenly, the surroundings started to shimmer, the colors melding, the boundaries blurring. The weightlessness of the dream realm gave way to a familiar grounding sensation.

"We're returning," I murmured, the dream realm receding like morning mist.

And as Elysium's sun pierced through our closed eyelids, we awoke in the Garden of Reverie, the whispers of the dreamscape still echoing in our ears. We returned with a profound realization: our dreams were not mere flights of fancy; they were the compass guiding our legacy.

As the members of our party gathered their senses in the Garden of Reverie, there was a peculiar alteration in the atmosphere, an almost imperceptible shift. The trees seemed to hum softly, and the petals of flowers shimmered in an unfamiliar, radiant hue.

Adolwolf, his eyes narrowed, muttered, "The dreamscape's resonance lingers stronger than before."

It was true. Never before had the transition between realms left such a lasting impact on Elysium. Yet, as we tried to understand this enigma, a more immediate oddity manifested: Clarissa's shadow, or rather the lack thereof.

Every being in Elysium cast a shadow, a silhouette formed by the dance of light and form. But where Clarissa stood, the ground lay untouched by her likeness.

Lyria, her voice a mere whisper, asked, "Clarissa, where is your shadow?"

Clarissa looked down, her face draining of color. "I... I don't know. It was there in the dreamscape." Panic edged her voice. "What has happened to me?"

Morphean, who had been silent post our re-entry, now stepped forth, his face betraying no emotion. "It is an anomaly, one that even I have not witnessed before. But fear not, it may yet be another layer of the dream's mystery, waiting to be unraveled."

"But how?" Clarissa's voice trembled, her usually calm demeanor replaced with rising fear. "How do I reclaim my shadow?"

"We must seek answers," I declared, looking to each face, noting the determination mirrored in their eyes. "If Elysium's dreamscape has taught us anything, it's that every mystery, every challenge, has a solution."

Adolwolf, always the pragmatist, inquired, "Morphean, do you have any records or ancient texts that speak of such phenomena? Even the most obscure of clues?"

Morphean hesitated, then nodded. "There exists an ancient tome, the 'Script of Shadows'. It speaks of the dance of light and darkness, the essence of form and void. Perhaps within its pages, we may find the answers we seek."

As the group agreed to embark on this new quest, a subtle yet undeniable connection was established amongst them, one that was not just of camaraderie but of divine purpose.

The path to the 'Script of Shadows' wasn't straightforward. It was believed to reside in the possession of the reclusive Seers of Silhouette, a group that had isolated themselves in the labyrinthine caverns known as the Echoing Abyss, a place where shadows danced to the rhythm of whispered tales.

In preparation, Morphean supplied us with a map, antiquated and intricate. The caverns, he explained, were a place where reality and illusion often blurred. The Seers used the distortions of the Echoing Abyss to mask their presence, and the journey would test our resolve, our faith in the intangible.

Chapter 6: In the Company of Shadows

As we descended into the caverns, the ambient light began to wane, the atmosphere growing cooler. Every echo, every footstep reverberated, creating a haunting symphony of sounds. The path split and twined like the roots of an ancient tree, and we relied heavily on the map, though its cryptic symbols and shifting lines often confounded more than guided.

It was during a particularly confusing juncture that Lyria, gazing upon one of the cavern walls, exclaimed, "Look! The shadows here, they seem... alive."

Indeed, the very shadows on the wall seemed to swirl and shape into forms: animals, elements, and abstract patterns. They danced, merged, and separated in a mesmerizing ballet. And then, as quickly as they had come alive, they settled back into mere dark patches on the cavern stone.

"It's a riddle," Adolwolf exclaimed. "I think the shadows are trying to communicate."

And he was right. As we ventured deeper, the shadows continued their performance, each time culminating in a distinct pattern, pointing us in a specific direction or indicating a course of action.

For days we navigated the labyrinth, solving shadowy enigmas, each clue drawing us closer to the Seers and the 'Script of Shadows'. Along the way, the bond between us deepened. Every challenge faced, every shadowy mystery unraveled, strengthened our collective resolve.

On the seventh day, we stumbled upon an expansive chamber bathed in an eerie blue luminescence. At its center stood a pedestal, upon which lay a leather-bound book- the 'Script of Shadows'.

But as Clarissa moved closer, a voice, both resonant and ethereal, echoed through the chamber. "Why do you seek the knowledge of shadows, dreamer without a silhouette?"

From the chamber's edges, figures draped in hooded cloaks stepped forward. Their eyes, pools of deep inky blackness, studied us intently.

"We are the Seers of Silhouette," another voice proclaimed. "You tread on sacred ground. Declare your intentions or face the consequences."

The chamber, bathed in its otherworldly glow, grew silent as the weight of the Seers' demand pressed upon us. Their eyes, reminiscent of the deepest abyss, bore into us, awaiting our reply.

"I seek my shadow," Clarissa responded, her voice unwavering despite her evident trepidation. "In the realm of dreams, amidst the interplay of legacy and hope, it vanished. And now, I stand incomplete, seeking answers from the very essence of the silhouette."

The Seers exchanged glances; their expressions hidden beneath their hoods. The chamber's silence was eventually broken by the voice of the Seer who had first addressed us.

"Many come seeking enlightenment in the realm of shadows, but few understand its true depth," the Seer intoned. "For a shadow is not merely an absence of light. It is a reflection of one's soul, a bridge to realms beyond comprehension."

Adolwolf, ever curious and rarely intimidated, inquired, "So you possess the knowledge to restore Clarissa's shadow?"

"The 'Script of Shadows' holds vast knowledge, encompassing secrets of the silhouette, from its birth to its end," another Seer elaborated. "But to harness that knowledge, one must first understand the essence of shadows."

The Seers motioned for us to sit in a circle around the pedestal holding the ancient tome. As we did, the room's luminescence seemed to breathe deeply, as if resonating with the very heartbeat of the cavern.

The lead Seer began to recite verses from the tome, "of birth and light in lands respite, of shadows death in dreams descent" and as the words flowed, the chamber was filled with vivid, shadowy apparitions. We witnessed the birth of Elysium, where light first met darkness, casting the realm's inaugural shadows. Tales of beings who had traversed realms, their shadows acting as anchors, unfolded. The narrative spun, detailing the interplay of light and shadow, and how each entity in Elysium was tethered to both realms.

As the seconds passed, a profound realization dawned upon us: shadows were not mere dark reflections. They were the soul's echo, a manifestation of one's essence, proof of existence across realms.

When the recitation concluded, the lead Seer posed a question: "Knowing now the gravity of what you seek, do you still wish to pursue the restoration of the lost shadow?"

Clarissa, her determination evident, nodded. "More than ever. For it isn't just a shadow I seek, but a piece of my very essence."

The Seers exchanged silent acknowledgments. "Then prepare, dreamer. For the path to reclaiming your shadow is intertwined with rediscovering yourself. You must journey to the Shadow Sanctum, where the very fabric of Elysium's essence converges. There, amidst realms of silhouette and luminescence, you will find your answers."

As we prepared for the journey to the Shadow Sanctum, the Seers provided provisions and elixirs believed to aid us in navigating the delicate balance between light and shadow. They warned of the challenges ahead, emphasizing that the Sanctum was a place of both immense power and profound vulnerability.

The journey was arduous, leading us through landscapes that defied comprehension. We traversed vast deserts where shadows moved like liquid beneath our feet, and dense forests where beams of light pierced through like sharp arrows.

It was in one such forest, where the dappled light played tricks on the eyes, that tragedy struck. We were ambushed. From the trees, ethereal wraith-like creatures descended, their forms constantly shifting between substance and shadow. We battled valiantly, our newfound understanding of shadows aiding in our defense. However, the wraiths were relentless and eerily silent, making their attacks all the more unnerving.

In the heat of the battle, Lyria, wielding an elixir gifted by the Seers, fashioned a barrier of light, providing us a momentary shield. It was then, in that brief moment of clarity, that she locked eyes with one of the wraiths. There was recognition, a fleeting moment where time seemed to stand still.

Lyria, her voice filled with disbelief, whispered a name from her past, a name she had shared with us around campfires – "Elowen?"

The wraith paused, and for a split second, the shadowy form seemed to coalesce into a more human shape, bearing a striking resemblance to Lyria's childhood friend, who she believed had been lost to the shadows years ago.

Before any of us could react, another wraith lunged at Lyria. Adolwolf, ever vigilant, stepped in its path to shield her, but the wraith's shadowy touch was chilling, draining life force with its cold embrace. With a heart-wrenching scream from Clarissa, Adolwolf fell, his once vibrant eyes now glazed and empty.

The world seemed to blur as grief and rage consumed us. Our retaliation was fierce. With renewed vigor and the raw emotion of loss fueling us, we managed to repel the wraiths, but the victory felt hollow.

As the battle's remnants cleared, the group gathered around Adolwolf, the weight of loss evident in every face. Clarissa, tears streaming, whispered words from an old Elysium hymn, her voice shaking with every note.

Lyria, on the other hand, was torn. The revelation about Elowen added layers of complexity to her grief. The lines between friend and foe, past and present, were becoming increasingly blurred.

The forest, once filled with the playful dance of light and shadow, now seemed to mourn with us. We had gained invaluable knowledge on our quest, but it came at a heartbreaking price. Our journey to the Shadow Sanctum was no longer just about Clarissa's missing silhouette; it was a pilgrimage of redemption, understanding, and, without a shadow of a doubt, healing.

The sun, once a brilliant beacon illuminating our path, now hung heavy and somber in the sky, casting elongated, melancholic shadows across the landscape. We set up a makeshift camp near a serene glade. The decision to give Adolwolf a proper farewell was unanimous.

Gathering around our fallen companion, Clarissa began to weave a protective circle with elements from our surroundings. Petals from twilight blossoms, sacred stones, and fragments of moonbeam silk formed a delicate perimeter. In the midst of our despair, it was essential to ensure that Adolwolf's spirit was free from the malevolent grasp of the shadows.

Lyria, her eyes red and swollen, took a deep breath and began to sing an old requiem. The hauntingly beautiful melody spoke of timelessness, love, loss, and the eternal dance between light and shadow. As her voice soared and dipped, filling the forest with its lament, Adolwolf's form began to shimmer, absorbing the luminescence of the glade.

Hours seemed like mere moments as we all shared stories of Adolwolf—his bravery, his wit, and the moments he offered solace. With each tale, a little more of him seemed to merge with the radiance around, turning it into a breathtaking spectacle of swirling lights.

As dawn approached, the final part of the ritual was at hand. Clarissa, holding a small vial of crystalline liquid given by the Seers, whispered, "May the shadows never bind you, and may your light forever shine, even in the darkest corners of Elysium."

She released the liquid into the air, where it sparkled and danced, intertwining with Adolwolf's luminous essence. Slowly, his form started rising, becoming one with the early morning mist, illuminating it from within. The forest seemed to breathe with us, echoing our sorrow and respect.

Exhausted, emotionally and physically, we decided to rest for a few hours before resuming our journey. While the others drifted into sleep, Lyria sat, lost in thought, occasionally glancing at the direction from which the wraiths had come. The revelation about Elowen haunted her. She needed answers.

When the first rays of the sun began to break, Clarissa approached Lyria. "This journey... it's becoming more complex than we ever imagined," she whispered. "But remember, in the realm of dreams and shadows, not everything is as it seems."

Lyria nodded, "I know. But Elowen... if there's even a fragment of her true self in that wraith, I need to find out. For her. For me."

The two women sat in quiet reflection, aware that as they ventured deeper into the mysteries of Elysium, they were also diving deeper into the enigma of their souls. The group, though diminished in number, grew stronger in resolve. They would face the Shadow Sanctum and its secrets, driven by love, legacy, and the undying hope of illumination.

> The next day after Adolwolf's ethereal departure, we resumed our journey, our steps weighed down by a mix of sorrow and determination. But even in the gravest of moments, Elysium's landscapes could still elicit a sense of wonder. The horizon shimmered with colors that defied description, casting the world in an enchanting play of light.

Yet, among the beauty, there lay a condensing tension. As the day drew on, Lyria found herself more and more entranced by the ancient forests and the stories they whispered through the breeze. Memories of the City of Sleep, once fuzzy and distant, began to resurface. There, in the depth of her mind, were fragments of Adolwolf and Elowen's shared dreams. Although she hadn't been a part of them, her connection to Elowen allowed her to perceive echoes of their shared past.

That night, as the moon hung luminous and full, Lyria sat Clarissa down by the campfire. The soft glow illuminated their faces as Lyria began to speak, her words a gentle river of memories. "I've been feeling... echoes, glimpses of the past that aren't mine. Dreams shared between Adolwolf and Elowen."

Clarissa, ever intuitive, nodded slowly. "The realm of dreams is a powerful one. Bonds forged there can leave imprints that traverse time and space."

"I think," Lyria hesitated, searching for the right words, "I think these dreams, these shared memories, hold a key. Elowen's transformation into a wraith wasn't merely a product of her own descent into darkness. It was intertwined with Adolwolf's journey, with their shared dreams. And it's no coincidence that we're all here now."

Their reflections were interrupted by a sudden rustling in the bushes. Out stepped Mirela, the enigmatic dream-weaver. Her eyes, pools of ever-changing hues, locked onto Lyria.

"You're on the precipice of understanding," Mirela intoned, her voice echoing the melodies of dreams. "The world you walk, the choices you make, are all connected to the realm of sleep. But beware," she added, her gaze turning steely, "for the shadows you chase are not just external. They lurk within, and understanding your past is only the first step in confronting them."

Before anyone could respond, Mirela vanished as mysteriously as she had appeared, leaving behind a trail of luminescent stardust. The night deepened, and we were left to contemplate the intertwining of dreams, destiny, and the shadows that lay ahead.

Chapter 7: The Quest for Shadow

The verdant expanse of Elysium was left behind, and the path ahead led into a land where contrasts were stark and every silhouette had a story. This was the threshold of the Shadow Sanctum, a place where every being's shadow held sway over its essence.

As we trekked on, the ambient light dimmed, not from the setting sun but from the profound density of the shadows around us. The trees bore an obsidian hue, their leaves rustling with whispers of old tales and secrets.

Clarissa's usually vibrant demeanor was tinged with apprehension. Her own journey here was deeply personal. Her shadow had been taken, separated from her. Without it, she felt incomplete, always on the verge of dissipating. It was a vulnerability she rarely showed, but Clarissa, Lyria and I were well aware, having vowed to aid in her quest.

I, with my affinity for arcane energies, could sense the distortions in the environment. "The Sanctum's heart is near," I murmured, my fingers tracing unseen patterns in the air. "Your shadow, Clarissa, it calls to you."

Lyria, her bond with Elowen amplifying her sensitivities, nodded. "It's more than just a shadow. It's a part of Clarissa's soul, her very essence. We must tread with caution."

We came upon a vast clearing where the ground shimmered like darkened glass, reflecting an inverted sky. At its center stood an ancient stone monolith, inscribed with runes that pulsed dimly.

From behind the monolith emerged a slender figure, draped in silver and gray. "Welcome to the heart of the Shadow Sanctum," she intoned. Her voice was melodic, yet it carried an underlying note of sorrow. "I am Nylara, Guardian of Lost Shadows. You seek to reclaim what was taken. But be warned, the path to reunification is not without its trials."

Clarissa, taking a deep breath, stepped forward. "I understand the risks, but I cannot continue to exist in this fragmented state. My shadow and my essence, must be rejoined."

Nylara appraised her with eyes that seemed to have witnessed eons. "Very well. But know that to reclaim your shadow, you must confront the reasons it was taken in the first place. Face your fears, your regrets, and your unspoken truths."

I and Lyria moved closer to Clarissa, our unity evident. We were ready to face the trials of the Sanctum together.

The monolith began to glow, its runes brightening as a portal slowly opened. Beyond it lay a realm of shifting landscapes and memories, where Clarissa's deepest fears and hopes roamed freely.

We, without hesitation rushed towards the monolithic portal now opening, hand in hand, and stepped into the unknown, determined to restore Clarissa's lost silhouette and confront the hidden truths of their intertwined fates.

The heart of the Shadow Sanctum was a place of paradoxes. The ground felt solid, yet it rippled like water with every step they took. The air was still, but it carried the whispered voices of countless souls who'd faced their innermost fears.

Surrounding Nylara were obsidian pillars, each inscribed with luminescent runes that danced and shifted with a rhythm of their own. At the very center, encased in a translucent crystal, was a silhouette — Clarissa's shadow, writhing as if trying to break free.

Clarissa took a step forward, her resolve evident. "I am ready."

Nylara, with a graceful wave of her hand, summoned an ethereal mirror that floated before Clarissa. The surface remained dark, devoid of any reflection. "To reclaim your shadow, you must first confront yourself," she instructed.

As Clarissa peered into the mirror, it began to shimmer, revealing a reflection not of her current self but of various versions of her from different points in her life. The innocent child in the market square, the lost teenager on the cliff, and countless others, each representing a memory, a choice, a regret.

With each reflection, Clarissa was forced to relive moments of pain, joy, love, and loss. She saw herself making choices she regretted, facing moments of weakness, but also instances of strength and resilience.

I, Clarissa, and Lyria, mere spectators to this deeply personal journey, could only offer silent support, our hands intertwined, drawing strength from each other.

As Clarissa faced each memory, the shadows around the crystal began to dissipate, its luminescence growing brighter. Yet, with each recollection, Clarissa's energy seemed to wane, the toll of confronting her past evident.

Finally, the mirror revealed the current Clarissa, the sum of all her experiences. She stared deep into her own eyes, taking in every detail. "I accept myself," she declared, her voice echoing throughout the sanctum. "Every flaw, every strength, every decision. They have made me who I am."

With that proclamation, the crystal shattered, releasing her shadow, which rushed towards her, merging with her in a blinding flash of light. Only to be separated again by the very flash it had created. When the luminescence faded, Clarissa stood incomplete once more, her shadow gone to another crystal within the Shadow Sanctum.

Nylara approached, a smile playing on her lips. "You have almost done what many could not. You have faced yourself in part. But your shadow is not yet yours."

Lyria and I rushed forward, enveloping Clarissa in a group embrace, our journey in the sanctum far from over. And the greater journey, with its twists, inversions, and revelations, was only just beginning.

Outside the Shadow Sanctum, the world seemed darker to Clarissa, as if a veil had been put over her eyes. Her shadow, an entity still separated, now longed to be in tandem with her. Knowing we had to retrieve her shadow was of the greatest importance, but other matters beckoned us.

TEROA

As we ventured forth, the landscape began to transform. Ancient trees with gnarled roots gave way to vast meadows filled with bioluminescent flora, their glow illuminating the path. In the distance, we could hear the soft murmurs of a brook, and a melody that sounded both haunting and familiar.

"Can you hear it?" Lyria whispered, her ears twitching. "The song... it's the old tune of the Elders."

I nodded. "Legends speak of the Elders' song. It's said to contain ancient truths, stories that predate even the sanctum."

Drawn to the melody, we found ourselves at the edge of a brook. Hovering above the water were ethereal figures, each one humming a part of the complex harmony. These were the spirits of the Elders, keepers of the world's oldest stories.

A spirit, distinguishable from the rest by its radiant aura, drifted towards Clarissa. "You," it began in a voice that was like a soft breeze, "have awakened an old tale, one that involves you more than you might believe."

Lyria and I exchanged glances, sensing that Clarissa's journey of self-discovery was far from over.

The Elder continued, "Long ago, in a dream realm separate from this, two souls met and forged a bond. A bond so powerful that it transcended realities."

Clarissa's heart raced. Memories from the depths of her subconscious began to surface, memories of a shared dream, where she was not alone.

"Was it... Adolwolf?" she hesitated, recalling their shared narrative.

The spirit nodded. "Adolwolf and you once knew each other in the world of dreams. Your souls connected, sharing dreams that shaped destinies. But with time, memories faded, and both of you forgot."

My brow furrowed, "But why is this relevant now?"

The spirit shimmered, "Because that bond, that shared dream, contains the key to facing the looming darkness ahead. Adolwolf is not just a mere companion in your journey; he is an integral part of your destiny."

Clarissa took a deep breath, processing the revelation. "So, what do we do next?"

The Elder spirit moved closer, its voice gentle yet insistent, "Find Adolwolf. Reconnect with the dreams of your past. Together, you will unlock the strength to confront the shadows that threaten not just you but the very fabric of this realm."

As the melody of the Elders grew fainter, we set our sights on our next destination, armed with newfound knowledge and a clearer purpose. The path ahead was uncertain, but the revelations from the past would light our way.

Meanwhile, Adolwolf, in his ethereal spirit form, having sensed the energies shifting after Clarissa's return from the Shadow Sanctum, had set up a camp near the edges of the Luminous Plains along the brook very near to us. His tent, constructed from woven moonbeams and sunrays, shimmered between reality and dreams. As he looked out upon his moonlit camp, we made our way along the brook. And in doing so we spotted a glowing camp in the distance. And upon seeing Clarissa, as we ventured closer, a myriad of emotions flitted across Adolwolfs face — surprise, joy, uncertainty.

"Clarissa," he uttered, voice tinged with the weight of unsaid words and forgotten memories.

She approached him, her shadow trailing smoothly behind her. "Adolwolf, there are things we need to discuss. Things about us that neither of us remembers clearly."

Seated by the flickering fire, whose flames danced to an otherworldly rhythm, Adolwolf began recounting a dream. "There was a citadel, floating amidst the clouds. Skies painted with hues of twilight, and a bridge, ethereal and glowing, connecting our worlds. You were there, and so was I."

Clarissa nodded, the memories beginning to solidify. "Yes, the Cloud Citadel. We'd meet there, crafting stories, dreaming of realities beyond our own. But why can't I recall it all?"

Adolwolf sighed, "Dreams, especially shared ones, reside on the precipice of reality and imagination. They're fragile. With time, they fray and fade."

Lyria, ever curious, posed a question. "But why did you two share such a dream? What was its purpose?"

Adolwolf gazed into the fire, lost in thought. "In that dream realm, Clarissa and I were Dreamweavers. Our role was to safeguard the balance between dreams and reality. We spun dreams so powerful, so vivid, they would occasionally bleed into the waking world."

My expression grew serious, "So, what happened?"

"The balance was disrupted," Adolwolf's voice was heavy. "There was a force, a shadowy entity, that sought to turn dreams into nightmares, blurring the lines between sleep and wakefulness. In a bid to stop it, we..." he trailed off, his gaze distant, "we made choices that separated our dream selves, ensuring that the entity was trapped in the dream realm. But it seems, it's found a way out."

Clarissa's heart raced; the implications clear. The challenges she'd faced, the journey to reclaim her shadow, were all connected to this ancient entity from the shared dream realm. "Then we need to restore the balance. Together."

Adolwolf nodded, determination lighting his eyes. "Our combined strength as Dreamweavers can fend it off. We just need to remember, to truly connect with our past selves."

Our unified group sat silently, contemplating the gravity of our mission. The night deepened; the stars above seemed to pulse in tandem with our resolve. We were not merely travelers on a quest; we were guardians of both dream and reality. The path ahead was nebulous, but one thing was clear — together, we would face the shadows of the past to ensure a brighter future.

As the hours passed, the campfire became a place of revelations and recollections. Each flickering flame seemed to unveil a forgotten fragment, a hazy memory, of the dream-filled nights in the Cloud Citadel. Lyria and I listened raptly, as the tapestry of Clarissa and Adolwolf's shared past unfolded.

"I remember a particular evening," Adolwolf began, eyes distant, "We stood atop the highest turret of the citadel, watching as stars transformed into ethereal birds, their melodies stitching together the fabric of dreams."

Clarissa smiled softly, "I remember that night too. Those melodies… they weren't just sounds; they carried emotions, experiences, histories. And we, as Dreamweavers, had to ensure they harmonized, to maintain the equilibrium of the dream realm."

Lyria, entranced by the tale, whispered, "That's beautiful. So, dreams aren't just fleeting images, they are narratives powered by emotions?"

I, feeling compelled, added, "And if dreams are powered by emotions, then nightmares would be…"

"…corrupted emotions," finished Adolwolf. "When the entity disrupted the dream realm, it was twisting emotions, casting shadows where there should've been light. Our task was not only to weave dreams but to purify those emotions, turning despair into hope, fear into courage."

"And that's the key!" Clarissa exclaimed, a realization dawning upon her. "Our journey, the trials we faced, they've been strengthening our emotional resilience. To face the entity, we need to be emotionally fortified, to prevent it from twisting our own emotions against us."

Adolwolf grasped Clarissa's hand, their shadows merging for a brief moment. "Then let's fortify each other. We can use the campfire as a conduit, revisiting our shared dreams, strengthening our bond, and preparing for the battle ahead."

As we sat in a circle, hands joined, our shadows intertwined. The fire crackled, its flames dancing higher, taking on hues of blue and purple. And as we closed our eyes, we found ourselves atop the Cloud Citadel once more, the world of dreams stretching endlessly before us.

There, in the realm of dreams, we trained and prepared. We faced our fears, relived our joys, and strengthened our bond. And when we finally opened our eyes, the first rays of dawn were breaking, casting the world in a golden hue.

I looked around, rejuvenated, "It felt like we spent an eternity in there."

Lyria nodded in agreement, her ears twitching in contentment. "Yet, only a night has passed here."

Adolwolf stood up, resolve clear in his eyes. "We're ready. The entity won't stand a chance against our united front."

Clarissa, feeling a connection to her past, her dreams, and her companions, declared, "Together, we'll ensure that dreams remain a beacon of hope. Let's move forward."

And with the rising sun as our guide, we set forth, ready to confront the shadows that lurked in the depths of dreams and reality alike.

Chapter 8: The Bridge Between Dreams

As we journeyed forth, the landscape began to change, taking on a otherworldly quality. Trees with silver bark and leaves that shimmered like stars lined our path. The air was heavy with a melodic hum, a resonance reminiscent of the harmonies from the Cloud Citadel. It was clear we were nearing the nexus where dreams and reality intertwined

"I've heard of this place," murmured Lyria, her eyes wide in wonder. "The Dreaming Glade. It's said to be where the veil between our world and the dream realm is thinnest."

Adolwolf nodded. "It is here we must confront the entity. But be cautious; the laws of physics and logic as we know them may not apply. Our emotions, our will, will shape the world around us."

Our path led us to a vast, tranquil lake. Its surface mirrored the cosmos above, stars twinkling from its depths. In the center stood a magnificent structure — a bridge made of luminescent strands, each glowing with its own light, representing individual dreams woven together.

"This is it," whispered Clarissa, "The Bridge of Dreams. We must cross it to reach the entity."

With each step across the bridge, the dreamscape around us shifted, presenting us with visions from our past, alternate realities, and unfulfilled desires. It was a maze of emotions and memories, each more disorienting than the last.

I found myself back in my childhood home, faced with the choice I regretted the most. Lyria saw an alternate path where her tribe had never been driven from their homeland. Clarissa and Adolwolf were presented with a life where they had never been separated, living out their days peacefully in the Cloud Citadel.

While these visions were tempting, offering us a chance to live out our deepest desires and rectify past regrets, we knew we couldn't stay. Holding onto each other, drawing strength from our shared bond, we waded through the sea of dreams, focused on our goal.

As we neared the end of the bridge, a dark maelstrom formed ahead, shadows swirling and coalescing into the form of the entity. It was a mass of writhing darkness, its form constantly shifting — a true embodiment of chaotic nightmares.

"You cannot stop me," it hissed, its voice echoing with a thousand whispers. "I am the culmination of every fear, every regret, every suppressed emotion. I am inevitable."

Adolwolf stepped forward, determination evident in his posture. "Perhaps. But you forget one thing. While nightmares are powerful, dreams of hope, love, and unity are stronger."

With that declaration, we united our energies, drawing from the positive emotions and memories we had fortified in the campfire ritual. A radiant light emanated from us, pushing back against the darkness of the entity.

The battle was one of wills, with the entity trying to drown us in despair while we countered with beams of hope, love, and unity. The Bridge of Dreams became a battleground of light and shadow, dream and nightmare.

As the conflict raged on, we realized that to truly defeat the entity, we needed to restore the disrupted balance between dreams and reality. Channeling our energies, we began to weave a new dream — a dream where the entity was not a malevolent force but a guardian, ensuring that dreams remained a safe haven.

It was a monumental task, reshaping the very essence of the entity. But with our combined strength and the collective dreams of countless souls backing us, we began to make headway. Slowly, the entity's form began to change, the darkness being replaced by a soft, luminescent glow.

With one final push, the transformation was complete. The entity, now a guardian of dreams, nodded in acknowledgment towards us.

"I understand now," the guardian sung, its voice soft and melodic. "Thank you."

With the entity's transformation and the balance restored, the Dreaming Glade returned to its tranquil state. We, having accomplished our mission, looked at each other with smiles of relief and pride.

Returning from the Dreaming Glade felt like emerging from a deep, restorative slumber. The world seemed brighter, more vivid. Trees swayed with newfound vitality, and even the wind carried a harmonious melody. The entity's transformation hadn't just affected the dream realm; its waves were felt in the waking world as well.

In the aftermath of our epic confrontation, we found a renewed purpose. With the entity now a guardian, there was a unique opportunity to bridge the worlds of dreams and reality further.

So, I began studying the fabric of dreams in greater detail. "There's so much potential here," I mused, my fingers tracing an intricate pattern in the air, representing the interwoven dreams of countless souls. "We could teach others to harness the power of dreams, turning them into tangible realities."

Lyria, inspired by the resilience of dreams, started chronicling our journey. Using her innate connection with nature, she etched stories into the barks of ancient trees and whispered tales to the winds, ensuring that the saga of our adventure would be carried to every corner of the world.

Adolwolf and Clarissa, with their shared past and deep understanding of the dream realm, established The Sanctuary of Solace — a place where Dreamweavers from all over could come, learn, and harness the power of dreams. It wasn't just a place of learning but also a refuge for those seeking solace in the embrace of dreams.

And so a peculiar phenomenon started to manifest. People across lands began recounting dreams that felt eerily familiar. Dreams of a radiant bridge connecting stars, of a tumultuous battle between light and shadow, of four figures standing tall against the encroaching darkness. It was as if the very essence of our adventure had seeped into the collective consciousness of the world.

That evening, as the first stars began to appear in the twilight sky, a young girl approached the sanctuary. She looked no older than ten, her eyes filled with wonder and curiosity. "I dreamt of this place," she whispered, clutching a small, intricately woven dreamcatcher. "And I dreamt of all of you."

Clarissa knelt beside the child, her eyes meeting the girl's. "And what did you see in your dream?"

The girl's voice was soft, almost a whisper, as she recounted a vision of a future where dreams and reality seamlessly merged, where every soul could shape their destiny, drawing from the boundless canvas of dreams.

Adolwolf, in his ethereal spirit form, looked at the young dreamer, and felt a surge of hope. Their journey, their battle, had not only saved the realm of dreams but had also ignited a spark, a beacon, that would guide countless souls in the times to come.

The sanctuary, now a luminous beacon in the darkness, pulsed with energy. The echoes of a dream, a dream of hope, unity, and boundless possibilities, reverberated across the lands, promising a brighter, dream-filled tomorrow.

With the arrival of the young dreamer, word spread like wildfire. People from all walks of life, touched by the echoes of our journey, began flocking to the sanctuary. They came with hope in their eyes, dreams in their hearts, and tales of shared visions.

Every evening, as the world succumbed to twilight, a gathering took place. Dreamers shared their stories, drawing parallels and marveling at the similarities. It wasn't just the events of our adventure that they dreamt of; new narratives emerged, stories that were continuations, offshoots, or alternate versions of the central tale.

One man spoke of a dream where he sailed on a luminescent sea, guided by starlight, to an island made entirely of clouds. Another recounted a vision of dancing with shadows, not as adversaries, but as partners, in a harmonious ballet. A woman shared a poignant tale where the entity, in its previous dark form, was not vanquished but was instead embraced, its fears and insecurities soothed by the collective love of the dream realm.

The sanctuary buzzed with the energy of the world's dreamers. With every shared tale, the fabric of dreams grew richer, denser. I, observing the phenomenon, termed it the "Dream Vector" - a focal point where the dreams of many converged, amplifying their essence.

Adolwolf, with his innate connection to the dream realm, felt the shifts more profoundly. He would often lose himself, wandering in the labyrinth of collective dreams. One evening, he returned from such a sojourn, a pensive look on his face.

"We're on the cusp of something monumental," he declared. "The dreams are not just tales or desires. They're precursors, blueprints. They're charting out potential futures, alternate realities."

Lyria, always in tune with the ebb and flow of nature, sensed it too. "The trees whisper of change," she conveyed, her fingers brushing the bark of an ancient oak. "The winds carry tales of futures yet to unfold."

The sanctuary, initially a place of learning, had transformed into something grander — a living, breathing tapestry of dreams. Every night, as dreamers gathered, their collective energies would spiral upwards, painting the night sky with auroras of many hues. It was a spectacle, a dance of dreams.

As the days passed, a lingering thought began to take root among the Dreamweavers. If dreams held the power to shape reality, then wasn't there a responsibility to ensure that the dreams that took root were ones of hope, love, and unity?

Clarissa, always the voice of reason, confronted the subject one evening. "Dreams are powerful, but they're also vulnerable," she began. "What if a dream of despair, of darkness, takes root? Would we not then be responsible for its manifestation in reality?"

The group and I pondered on this, realizing the weight of our newfound role. We weren't just guardians or teachers; we were stewards of the future. The question remained: how does one nurture dreams, ensuring they lead to a brighter, harmonious future?

And so we sat in contemplation, the weight of our responsibility heavy on our shoulders, knowing that the path ahead, much like the world of dreams, was uncertain and filled with endless possibilities.

As I gazed upon the mesmerizing tapestry of dreams, the glow from the gathered souls illuminating the sanctuary, I couldn't help but feel an odd mixture of awe and trepidation. The patterns swirling before us weren't just representations of desires and hopes; they were imprints of souls, each telling a unique tale, each holding a universe of its own.

I remember the days when my studies of dreams were mere theory, confined to dusty old books and whispered legends. Now, surrounded by their tangible presence, the gravity of our role weighed on me. Clarissa's words echoed in my mind. How could we possibly navigate such a vast realm of possibilities and ensure the balance was maintained?

"Rhineheart," Adolwolf's voice broke through my reverie, his eyes reflecting a depth of understanding, "I sense your unease. The world of dreams has always been your domain of study, and now you stand at its very heart."

I nodded, words momentarily escaping me. "It's just... overwhelming," I finally managed. "The infinite potential, the vast expanse of it all. How do we even begin to steward such a domain?"

Adolwolf smiled, his gaze turning back to the dream tapestry. "By understanding that we are but a part of it, not its masters. We guide, we nurture, but we do not control."

Lyria, her fingers gently caressing a shimmering thread, added, "Dreams, like nature, have a way of finding balance. We must trust in that."

As the night deepened, I found myself wandering the sanctuary, lost in thought. My steps brought me to a secluded alcove where a small fountain murmured softly. Seated by its edge was the young dreamer who had come to us days ago, her eyes reflecting the moonlight.

She looked up as I approached, her gaze piercing yet gentle. "You wonder how to guide the dreams," she whispered, as if reading my very soul.

I sat down beside her, the cool water of the fountain lending a calming ambiance. "Yes," I admitted. "It's a responsibility unlike any other."

The girl, playing with her dreamcatcher, responded, "Dreams are like this," she held up the intricate weave, "a delicate balance of threads. Pull too hard, and it distorts. Let it flow, and it finds its form."

I contemplated her words, the wisdom far beyond her years evident. "But how do we ensure that the form it takes is one of hope and not despair?"

She smiled, a serene expression on her young face. "By dreaming, Rhineheart. By believing. The essence of dreams is belief. If you and the others believe in a brighter tomorrow, so shall it be."

Chapter 9: Tower Obsidian

The days following our profound realizations were a whirlwind of activity. The sanctuary thrummed with life and dream-energy. People came and went, sharing tales, experiencing shared dreams, and leaving with renewed hope.

One particular evening, as the sanctuary was bathed in the silvery light of the moon, a curious event transpired. A series of dreams echoed through the collective tapestry, each dreamer experiencing the same vision simultaneously. The dream was of a magnificent city built on the clouds, its spires reaching the stars, with pathways of gold and silver.

A large obsidian tower stood at the city's center, an anomaly in the otherwise radiant landscape. From this tower, an eerie hum resonated, its vibrations felt even in the waking world.

As dreamers awoke from this collective vision, the energy in the sanctuary shifted. It was evident to all that this dream held significance, so my companions and I convened to decipher its meaning.

Lyria was the first to speak, her voice echoing the unease we all felt. "This dream... it's not just a manifestation of shared hope or desire. It is calling from somewhere outside of the collective."

Adolwolf nodded in agreement. "I sensed an ancient energy emanating from that obsidian tower. It's as if it beckons us, guiding us towards it."

Clarissa, her mind analyzing, postulated, "Could it be a confluence point, a nexus where dream realms converge? Or perhaps a challenge for us as stewards?"

My own mind raced with possibilities. The teachings of the old Dreamweavers hinted at realms beyond our comprehension, intersections of dreams and reality. "This city, this dream, might be a threshold," I pondered aloud. "It could represent an opportunity or a test. We must venture into it, discern its purpose."

As the decision solidified, preparations began. The sanctuary became a hub of activity. Dreamcatchers were crafted, obscure scrolls consulted, and rituals performed. If we were to venture into this shared dream, we needed to be prepared.

The chosen night arrived swiftly. The four of us, along with a few seasoned dreamers, sat in a circle, the air heavy with anticipation. Lyria began a soft chant, her voice weaving a protective shield around us. Adolwolf lit a series of incense, its smoke curling and dancing, creating a portal to the dream realm.

As the world around me blurred, I took a deep breath, anchoring myself to the essence of the dream. The sensation was akin to diving into a deep, vast ocean, but instead of water, I was surrounded by the ethereal substance of dreams.

Suddenly, the luminous city from our shared dream materialized before us. Its beauty was breathtaking, the spires shimmering, the pathways glowing. Yet, the obsidian tower loomed, casting a shadow over the dream realm.

We ventured forth, drawn inexplicably to the tower. As we approached its entrance, an inscription became visible, etched in a script that seemed to shift and change with every glance.

"To those who seek to understand the essence of dreams, know this: Dreams are not just visions; they are echoes of the soul. To embrace their true power, one must face the shadows within."

I exchanged glances with my companions, realizing that this journey was about to challenge us in ways we hadn't foreseen. The tower beckoned, its mysteries waiting to be unraveled. And with determination in our hearts, we stepped forth into the unknown.

The interior of the tower was as perplexing as its exterior. The walls, though made of dark obsidian, shimmered with iridescent colors. Spiraled staircases wound upwards, seemingly infinite, while other pathways branched into corridors that defied the laws of physics.

Lyria, ever sensitive to the energies around her, whispered, "This place is an enigma. Every stone, every pathway is imbued with memories, dreams, and shadows."

Clarissa reached out and touched one of the walls. "It's alive," she murmured, her usually analytical demeanor replaced with wonder. "The dreams of countless souls are embedded here."

Adolwolf studied the stairways, his fingers tracing patterns in the air. "The way up is a labyrinth. The tower tests our resolve, our very understanding of the dream realm."

"I think," I began, trying to find the right words, "that this isn't just about navigating the tower. It's about navigating our own inner worlds. We must face our shadows, confront our fears, and recognize our desires."

Adolwolf nodded. "Each of us will face a unique journey, even if we walk the same path."

Without any clear direction, we chose one of the spiral staircases, hoping it would lead us to the heart of the tower. The ascent was disorienting. Sometimes it felt like we were climbing downwards or walking on walls. Dreams and memories flitted around us—whispers of lost loves, ambitions, fears, and hopes.

Lyria suddenly stopped; her eyes distant. Before her materialized a vision of a younger self, laughing and playing in a sunlit meadow. It was a memory, one filled with innocence and joy. But as we watched, dark clouds gathered, and the young Lyria's laughter turned to sobs.

Lyria's voice trembled as she spoke, "This is the day my village was destroyed, the day I lost my family." She took a shaky breath. "I've never been able to revisit this memory without pain."

Clarissa gently grasped her hand. "We are with you, Lyria."

But as Lyria faced her traumatic past, the vision shifted. The clouds receded, and in their place stood figures made of light—her family, reaching out to her, their expressions loving and understanding. The pain of the memory remained, but it was now tempered with love and acceptance.

As we continued our ascent, each of us faced similar trials. I saw fragments of my past, moments of doubt and fear, but also of love and joy. With every step, the tower revealed more of our innermost selves.

Hours or perhaps days seemed to pass. Time was a fickle thing within the tower. Finally, we reached a vast chamber at the tower's pinnacle. In its center stood a crystalline dais, upon which pulsed a radiant orb—a nexus of dreams.

Approaching the orb, I felt a rush of emotions, memories, and dreams from countless souls, including my own. They intertwined, telling a collective story of humanity—its triumphs, its downfalls, its hopes.

"We've reached the heart," Clarissa whispered, tears glistening in her eyes.

Adolwolf, his voice filled with reverence, added, "And now, we must ensure it continues to beat, to dream."

We stood around the nexus for what felt like both an eternity and a fleeting moment, absorbing the weight of our experiences and revelations. The knowledge gained wasn't just personal; it expanded our understanding of the dream realm and its interconnectedness with the tangible world.

Adolwolf suddenly straightened, his eyes distant. "There's an energy shift," he said, "The tower is... settling."

Lyria nodded in agreement. "The balance is restored for now, but we need to ensure it remains this way."

As we descended the tower, the staircases and corridors that had once defied logic now seemed harmonious. Every twist and turn that had presented a challenge was now a welcome reminder of our internal growth.

Upon reaching the base, we were met by an unexpected sight. The once solitary tower was now surrounded by a multitude of dreamers. Word had spread throughout the dream realm about our ascent, drawing souls eager to experience their own journey of self-discovery.

Among the crowd, a familiar face approached. Elowen, her ethereal aura glowing more brilliantly than ever, stepped forth. "You've done it," she whispered, her voice brimming with pride. "You've not just ascended the tower but shown countless others the path."

Clarissa smiled softly. "It was never just about us. It's about everyone who dares to dream, to confront their fears, and seek understanding."

I gazed at the sea of expectant faces, their eyes alight with curiosity, hope, and determination. "We've unlocked a path," I mused, "But each journey will be unique, each revelation personal."

Elowen nodded, "And that is the beauty of dreams. They are as diverse and intricate as the souls who dream them."

Returning to the sanctuary, we were surprised to find it expanded to accommodate the influx of dreamers. Workshops were established, guided dream sessions initiated, and the collective energy was harnessed to bolster the dream realm's strength.

Amidst the joy and renewed hope, a gnawing feeling persisted in the pit of my stomach. Our ascent had revealed much, but I couldn't shake off the feeling that there was more—hidden layers, challenges, and truths waiting to be uncovered.

TEROA

One evening, as the sanctuary was bathed in twilight's soft glow, I sat atop a serene hill, my thoughts swirling like the colors of the setting sun. The realm of dreams was vast, intricate, and mysterious. And though we had achieved much, the journey was far from over.

From behind, a gentle hand rested on my shoulder, pulling me from my introspection. I turned to find Lyria, her eyes reflecting the sky's hues. "It's never truly over, is it?" she whispered.

I shook my head, smiling wryly. "No, but perhaps that's the beauty of it. The dream realm, much like life, is an ever-evolving tapestry, and we are but threads in its grand design."

Together, we gazed into the horizon, ready for whatever dreams or challenges lay ahead.

Those days following our ascent of the tower were vibrant, pulsing with an energy that was vitalizing. Dreamers from all corners of the realm came to learn, to explore, and to face their own truths. The sanctuary, once a secluded haven, thrived with more and more activity. And the nexus at the obsidian tower's peak became a beacon, a symbol of hope and personal growth.

But with every influx of energy, we realized that balance must be maintained. While the dream realm flourished, the waking world started showing signs of strain. News reached us of erratic weather patterns, inexplicable phenomena, and people waking up feeling more exhausted than when they'd gone to sleep.

Adolwolf, intrigued, was the first to draw the connection. "The two worlds, the dream realm and the waking realm, they coexist in a delicate balance. Our work here might be causing ripples in the tangible world."

Elowen, joining our discussion, added, "Dreams are not just idle fantasies. They are reflections, reactions to the waking world. They are energy, and energy can't be created or destroyed, only transferred."

I looked between the two, concern building within me. "Are we harming the waking world by bolstering the dream realm?"

Clarissa, always the voice of reason, replied, "We've brought attention to the dream realm, made it more vibrant. But maybe in doing so, we've drawn too much from the other side."

"We need to find a way to restore the balance," Lyria voiced, her brow furrowed in thought.

Determined to set things right, our group, along with Elowen and some of the most adept dreamers, began researching ways to channel the excess energy back into the waking world. While the dream realm was vast and mysterious, the waking world, with its own sets of rules and constraints, was equally intricate.

During our research, I stumbled upon an ancient text speaking of 'The Veil,' a boundary separating the dream realm from the waking world. The Veil, it seemed, wasn't just a metaphorical barrier but a tangible one, weaving through both worlds, keeping them in harmony.

"We need to find The Veil," I declared that evening. "It might be the key to restoring balance."

But the search for The Veil was as arduous as our ascent of the obsidian tower. It led us through forgotten corners of the dream realm, past visions of old worlds and futures not yet realized.

As we traversed a dreamscape resembling a dense forest, the atmosphere changed. The air grew heavier, the colors less vivid. As we walked, the dream trees gave way to a shimmering, translucent barrier pulsing with energy—The Veil.

Approaching it, I felt a pull, a connection to the waking world. The energy from the dream realm flowed towards The Veil, trying to seep through, but it was distorted, congested.

Adolwolf looked on with awe. "This is it. This is where the balance has been upset. We need to clear The Veil, let the energies flow naturally."

Pooling our knowledge and abilities, we began the task of restoring The Veil. Each of us contributed in our own way—Lyria sang melodies that harmonized with the frequencies of The Veil, Clarissa invoked old spells, Adolwolf traced ancient symbols in the air, and I focused on channeling the excess energy, guiding it towards The Veil.

As time, relative to our perception of it, passed, slowly the congestion began to clear. The dream realm's vibrant energy began to trickle back into the waking world, restoring the balance.

Exhausted yet fulfilled, we stepped back from The Veil, admiring our work. The boundary shimmered, now a healthy conduit between two worlds.

"The balance is restored," Elowen murmured with a smile.

But as we prepared to leave, a whisper reached my ears—a voice, ethereal and ancient. "Thank you," it murmured, "But remember, balance is a continuous act. The realms are forever intertwined, influencing one another."

I nodded silently, understanding the weight of our responsibility. We were not just dreamers; we were guardians, protectors of the balance between realms. And our journey was far from over.

The days that followed our repair of The Veil were serene, or at least as serene as they could be in a realm as mercurial as this. We decided to return to the obsidian tower, our makeshift headquarters, to regroup and decide our next steps. As guardians of the balance, it was now our duty to ensure that the dream realm and the waking world coexisted harmoniously.

While most days were consumed with maintaining the balance, the evenings were spent in camaraderie, exchanging stories of our adventures and explorations. I began to grow closer to Clarissa during these times. We shared an unspoken bond, an understanding that we were both searching for something deeper in this vast world of dreams.

One evening, as the last rays of the setting dream-sun bathed the tower in a golden hue, Clarissa pulled me aside. "Rhineheart," she began hesitantly, "Do you remember the first time we met, in the marketplace of that dream town?"

I nodded, remembering the vivid colors, and the bustling crowd. "Of course I do, now. It feels like ages ago, and perhaps it was."

She bit her lip, her gaze distant. "There's something I never told you about that day. When I first laid eyes on you, I had a vision, a premonition of sorts."

I leaned in closer, intrigued. "What did you see?"

Clarissa looked deep into my eyes. "I saw us, standing at the edge of a great abyss. And in that abyss, I saw shadows, countless shadows, all reaching out for us, pulling us in. But amidst the chaos, there was a single point of light. And I knew, somehow, that we were meant to find it, together."

I was taken aback. An abyss of shadows? A point of light? What did it all mean? As if reading my thoughts, Clarissa continued, "I think our journey with The Veil was just the beginning.

There's something more, something we're yet to discover. And that abyss, I believe it's our next destination."

"But why didn't you tell me sooner?" I inquired.

She hesitated for a moment. "I wasn't sure what it meant initially. But now, with everything that's happened, I think we're being guided towards a greater purpose."

The idea was daunting, but if my experiences in the dream realm had taught me anything, it was to trust my instincts and the connections I'd formed. If Clarissa believed this was our next step, then I was ready to embark on the journey, wherever it might lead.

Gathering our team once again, Clarissa and I shared her vision. With the same determination that had driven us to restore The Veil, we set out to uncover the mystery of the abyss and the point of light.

The days turned into a blur as we prepped for our journey into the abyss. Though Clarissa and I led the charge, every member of our party had a role to play. Lyria was our compass, sensing and guiding us through the ebb and flow of dream energies. Adolwolf, with his knack for lore, buried himself in books and scrolls, trying to find any mention of this abyss and its mysterious light.

But it was during one of our strategy sessions that Elowen, usually so quiet, spoke up. "I've been to the edge once," she said softly, her usually pale face tinged with a shade of deep blue, an indicator of her discomfort. We all turned towards her, surprised. "Not by choice," she quickly added. "But I've felt the pull of the shadows, heard their whispers."

I met her gaze. "What did they say?"

She looked away, struggling with the memory. "Promises of power, of understanding the true nature of dreams. But it wasn't just the words. It was the emotion, the seductive pull. It's alluring, in the most dangerous way. And once they have you, they won't let go."

The weight of her words settled over us. The journey ahead wasn't just one of discovery; it was one of survival. But Elowen's revelation was a gift — forewarned is forearmed.

Night fell, and I found myself unable to sleep. I made my way to the top of the tower, seeking solitude and perhaps a momentary escape from the heavy responsibility that now rested on our shoulders. As I looked out over the dream realm, a sea of stars spread out before me, twinkling and shimmering, each a beacon in the darkness.

Lost in thought, I barely noticed Clarissa joining me. "Beautiful, isn't it?" she whispered.

I nodded. "It's a reminder that even in the darkest of times, there's always a glimmer of hope."

She leaned into me, seeking comfort. "Rhineheart, are we doing the right thing? The abyss is unknown, and we've seen what it can do."

I took a deep breath. "I believe we are. This journey, it's bigger than us. We have a duty, not just to ourselves, but to every dreamer out there. We must find that point of light."

Clarissa looked up, determination shining in her eyes. "Then let's ensure we shine brighter than any shadow that tries to engulf us."

The following morning, with resolve in our hearts and hope as our guide, we ventured forth to face the abyss and its many mysteries. The path ahead was uncertain, but together, we were ready to brave the unknown.

Days turned into nights and nights merged back into days, the landscape changed. Gone were the familiar floating islands and vivid dreamscapes. The horizon darkened, and a cold chill set in. It was as if the entire realm was warning us of the impending abyss.

One evening, as we set up camp amidst the half-lit murkiness, Adolwolf approached me with a forgotten old tome. "I found something," he said, his eyes gleaming with that familiar scholarly excitement.

Flipping the pages to an age-worn illustration, he pointed to a series of symbols surrounding an eerily depicted abyss. "These symbols, they're not just decorative. They're a protective chant. It speaks of a ritual to guard one's mind against the shadows."

The thought of an added protection was undoubtedly appealing. We decided to gather around the fire that night and, under Adolwolf's guidance, practiced the chant until it was committed to memory. The melody was haunting but comforting, and as our voices rose in unison, the camp seemed brighter, the weight of our journey momentarily lifted.

Lyria, however, was growing restless. Her sensitivity to the dream energies meant she felt the pull of the abyss more profoundly than any of us. "It's like a siren call," she murmured to me one night, her normally vibrant eyes now clouded with worry. "And it's getting stronger."

Days later, we stood at the precipice. The vast expanse of the abyss stretched out before us, an endless void. The whispers Elowen had spoken of were now audible, a cacophony of voices that promised power and knowledge. But among them, there was a faint, melodic hum, like a lighthouse guiding ships away from danger.

"Remember the chant," Adolwolf reminded us. With a deep breath, we began our descent.

The shadows reached for us, their cold tentacles attempting to ensnare our minds. But the protective chant acted as a barrier. The further we went, the louder we chanted, and slowly but surely, the point of light Clarissa had seen in her vision began to grow clearer.

It wasn't until we reached a seemingly ancient platform that we realized the true nature of this place. In the center stood a pedestal, and upon it, a crystal that emitted a soft, radiant light. This was the source of the hum, the beacon amidst the chaos.

I stepped forward, drawn to the crystal. Touching it, memories flooded my mind—memories not of my own but of dreamers long past. Their hopes, fears, love, and losses. It was overwhelming but beautiful. The crystal wasn't just a beacon; it was a repository of dreams, a testament to the legacy of those who'd dreamt before us.

"We need to protect it," Clarissa whispered, echoing my thoughts. "If this falls into the wrong hands, the balance between realms could be lost forever."

It was clear to us now. Our journey had not been just about discovery but also about safeguarding a legacy, ensuring that the dreams of countless souls lived on.

But as we prepared to make our ascent back, a chilling realization struck us—while we were shielded from the shadows, the crystal was not. We had to find a way to protect it, and fast. The true challenge had only just begun.

From the very edges of the platform, the shadows began creeping in, drawn to the radiant energy of the crystal. They whispered promises of power, urging us to surrender the beacon, but our group was united, our resolve unbreakable.

Elowen, with her connection to the dream realm, began weaving a protective barrier around the platform. It shimmered like moonlight, keeping the shadows at bay. Lyria, using her innate sense of the energies, began channeling the power of the crystal, amplifying its beacon and pushing back the encroaching void.

Adolwolf, always our source of knowledge, quickly searched his tome. "There's a way to merge the chant with the dream energies," he exclaimed. "But it'll require all our voices, combined with the power of the crystal."

We stood in a circle around the crystal, hands joined, grounding ourselves. Clarissa began the chant, her voice confident and unwavering, and soon, the rest of us joined in. The melody resonated with the energy of the crystal, and an intricate web of light began to form around it.

The shadows, though numerous and persistent, were slowly receding. But just when victory seemed within our grasp, a deep, resonant voice echoed through the abyss, chilling us to our core.

"Such futile efforts," it boomed. "The shadows are eternal, while you are but fleeting dreams."

From the very heart of the abyss, a figure emerged, darkness personified. It was neither human nor creature but a manifestation of the void itself. Our protective barrier strained against its presence, threatening to shatter.

The entity reached out, its hand just inches away from the crystal, when suddenly, a bolt of pure dream energy shot forth, repelling it. I looked to my side and saw Clarissa, her eyes glowing with the same radiant light as the crystal, her very being connected to the dreams of countless souls.

"You may be of the abyss," she declared, "but we are of the dream. And dreams, though fragile, have the power to push back the night."

With a collective effort, and Clarissa at the forefront, we unleashed the combined power of the crystal and our own dream energies. The entity, caught off guard, was swept back into the abyss, its menacing voice echoing one last promise of return.

The immediate threat was over, but the battle had taken its toll. The platform, though intact, was forever marked by the shadows. The crystal, though still radiant, had dimmed slightly.

"We must return," Lyria whispered, her energy almost depleted. "This place, while wondrous, is not meant for us to linger."

Chapter 10: Resonance of Reverie

The days after our harrowing escape from the inky recesses of the abyss felt strangely introspective. Each of us, though immersed in the shared experience, seemed enveloped in our own reveries. The route meandered through a woodland, ethereal in nature, with trees radiating a gentle luminescence, mirroring the soft glimmer of half-remembered dreams.

As we advanced, an ineffable aura hung in the air—a mélange of forgotten hopes, ambitions, and tales from epochs long past. The very wind that rustled the luminescent leaves seemed to whisper the chronicles of ancient dreamers.

Adolwolf, with his predilection for the arcane, meticulously documented each anomaly we encountered. His tome now felt like both a compass and a repository of knowledge from this surreal realm. During one such introspective moment, a curious glade unveiled itself.

Dominating its heart was an imposing stele, adorned with glyphs eerily reminiscent of those from the abyssal chasm. The monolith emitted with a soft glow, and as we drew near, a palpable frisson permeated the atmosphere, causing the fabric of time itself to quiver.

Elowen, with her countenance awash with trepidation, spoke softly, "There's a familiarity here—a resonance not just with the dream realm but within our very souls." She turned her gaze to Adolwolf, a question unspoken yet understood, "Have our paths crossed this point before?"

He ruminated for a moment, weighing her words. "Not within this plane, perhaps. But dreams—they have an uncanny knack for braiding fates, intertwining souls in patterns too intricate for mortal comprehension."

Inexplicably drawn, I approached the stele, and the moment my fingers brushed its cold surface, a deluge of memories—ethereal, not my own—engulfed me. Vignettes flashed: a youthful Adolwolf, deeply engrossed in esoteric tomes, under the tutelage of a venerable mentor; Lyria, in another epoch, twirling ecstatically under a dreamy moon; and Elowen, standing resolutely where we now stood, her visage etched with determination.

But it was the image of Clarissa and me that lingered—the two of us, not as mere wanderers of this dreamscape but sovereigns of a vast, illustrious domain, our shared narrative the stuff of legends.

As the echo of these memories receded, I found myself tethered back to the present, the faces of my companions reflecting a blend of astonishment and recognition.

"It's an anchor," Elowen whispered, emotion evident in her voice. "A nexus where past, present, and potentialities collide."

Clarissa, her alabaster complexion betraying her emotions, clutched my hand tightly. "Our journey—it's preordained. Our fates, they're not merely coincidental but woven together, steered by the very dreams we tread."

With this, we knew that our odyssey in this enigmatic realm had a way of diverging into paths that seemed at the same time familiar yet anew. As stewards of these dreamscapes, destiny beckoned, and we were ready to heed its call.

I continued to find myself entranced by the monolithic stele's intricate glyphs, almost as if they whispered age-old secrets directly into my soul. Each marking seemed to resonate with the rhythm of the universe, pulsating to the heartbeat of all dreamers.

"My ancestors once spoke of such places," Adolwolf murmured, breaking the silence, his eyes fixated on the stele. "Realms where the boundaries between dream and reality blur. They believed that understanding such symbols could potentially unlock the latent power within a dreamer."

Lyria, her face a canvas of wonder, reached out hesitantly to touch the stone, fingers dancing lightly over the engraved symbols. A soft melody emanated, harmonizing with the soft glow that surrounded us. It was a song neither of us recognized, yet it felt nostalgically familiar, like an old lullaby heard in childhood.

Elowen, being the most attuned to the nuances of the dream realm, seemed to decipher a pattern. "There's a sequence, a rhythm to these glyphs. They aren't just static symbols; they're a story, a song, a guide."

And then, like the subtle weaving of a tapestry, the true purpose of our journey began to unravel before us. If we could learn this ancient song, interpret its story, perhaps we could harness its power, not just to traverse the dreamscape, but to shape it. We could restore what had been fragmented. And truly reclaim Clarissa's shadow.

Clarissa's grip tightened around my arm, her excitement palpable. "Rhineheart, think about it. If we could truly understand and control the realm of dreams, we might be able to restore lost memories, lost moments. And lost shadows. Not just for ourselves, but for others too."

I pondered her words, the implications vast and overwhelming. If dreams were the footprints of our soul, then controlling them was tantamount to touching the very essence of existence. But with such power came responsibility, and the potential for irrevocable consequences.

As the weight of our discovery settled, I realized that this journey was not just about personal redemption or reclamation. It was about understanding the delicate balance between power and purpose, between dreaming and awakening. The dream realm had beckoned us, and now, with a newfound purpose, we would answer its call.

The illumination from the stele began to diminish as we pulled ourselves from its magnetism. Yet the power we felt, the stories it told, had embedded themselves deeply within us.

"We need to tread carefully," I began, feeling an innate urge to protect the group from any unseen dangers. "While the promise of harnessing such a power is tempting, we can't forget the shadows that lurk, waiting to ensnare us."

Clarissa nodded in agreement; her fingers still intertwined with mine. "The balance is fragile. We've already seen how our actions ripple throughout this realm."

Adolwolf, flipping through the pages of his tome, paused, tapping a particularly weathered page adorned with illustrations eerily reminiscent of our surroundings. "According to the legends, there exists a sanctuary, a realm within the dreamscape untouched by time. The Ancients called it the 'Sanctum of Serenity.' It is said to be the heart of the dream realm, the origin of all dreams and, perhaps, the key to understanding the power we've uncovered."

Elowen's gaze intensified. "It's more than just a place, isn't it? It's a state of being, a point of pure equilibrium where dream and reality are in perfect harmony."

Lyria, who had been uncharacteristically silent, whispered, "Then that's where we must go. But we must remember, it's not just about reaching the sanctum, but about understanding its essence, its purpose."

As the words settled, a shift occurred. The luminescent forest around us began to hum, and the path ahead, previously concealed, revealed itself—illuminated by a gentle, ethereal glow, beckoning us to continue our quest.

Our journey through the dreamscape intensified. We encountered an array of dream states, each one a reflection of countless souls' hopes, desires, fears, and memories. Some were breathtaking in their beauty—vast meadows filled with radiant flowers, shimmering under a perpetual twilight. Others, however, were nightmares given form, twisted labyrinths echoing with sorrow and regret.

Yet, with each realm we traversed, our bond grew. The shared experiences, the challenges faced, and the mysteries unraveled intertwined our fates more tightly. It became evident that our individual strengths—Elowen's intuition, Adolwolf's knowledge, Lyria's empathy, Clarissa's determination, and my own resolve—were the very keys to navigating this intricate tapestry of dreams.

And as the Sanctum of Serenity drew closer, the weight of our mission became ever clearer. The balance between dream and reality, hope and despair, was in our hands. The dreamscape had chosen us, and we were ready to rise to the challenge. But with every step, the shadows grew restless, and an impending confrontation loomed.

The dreamscape, in all its whimsical splendor, could not have prepared us for the arduous path that lay ahead. Though our journey had been adorned with wonders and fascinations, a looming unease began to permeate the group. The Sanctum of Serenity, that hallowed heart of dreams, was our ultimate goal, and every step toward it bore a weight of anticipation.

"The closer we get," Clarissa murmured as we navigated through a valley where the air shimmered with vivid colors, "the more I feel the pull of the Sanctum of Serenity, but also, even more so from the Shadow Sanctum. But also...a resistance."

Adolwolf adjusted the satchel that bore his ancient tome. "The sanctums are a reservoir of immense energy, and like any powerful beacon, it attracts both light and darkness. We must be prepared for whatever lies in wait."

A sudden gust of wind rippled through the valley, carrying with it the soft lilt of voices. Elowen, with her preternatural sensitivity to the realm's energies, paused and tilted her head, eyes closed, trying to discern the source.

"It's the very essence of the dreamscape," she whispered, her voice tinged with awe. "The collective voices of countless souls, both living and departed, seeking solace, understanding, and purpose."

Lyria's gaze drifted skyward, where ephemeral wisps danced, each one representing a dream or memory. "It's beautiful," she said, her voice hushed, "but also...overwhelming. So many emotions, desires, regrets."

I felt it too—the sheer magnitude of collective consciousness that swirled around us, a symphony of human experience. It was humbling, realizing the vastness of the universe and the intricate dance of dreams that shaped our existence.

"We should set up camp here," I suggested, looking around for a suitable location. "It's important we're rested and centered before we approach the sanctum."

A soft clearing, bathed in a gentle, luminous glow, caught my eye. The ground was covered in a blanket of iridescent petals, creating a dreamlike ambiance—perfect for our reprieve.

As night enveloped our temporary abode, Adolwolf began to recite ancient verses, while Lyria played a haunting melody on a flute fashioned from dreamflowers and wonderstone. It was a surreal scene, reminding us all of the ethereal beauty that existed in this realm.

But as sleep claimed us, my dreams were not of wonder and hope but of forewarning. Shadowy figures loomed on the horizon, and an ancient voice echoed, "Beware the heart's desire, for it may not be what it seems."

As dawn began to paint the dreamscape in hues of lavender and gold, we gathered, readying ourselves for the impending day's challenges. The dreamtide—this realm's version of dawn—held a peculiar calm. The chorus of countless voices was momentarily hushed, giving way to a fleeting moment of stillness.

Elowen, her hair shimmering like a cascade of moonbeams, drew a circle in the iridescent sand. "This is an ancient ritual," she began, her voice resonant and soothing, "It's a way to center ourselves, to draw strength from the dreamscape and fortify our resolve."

Each of us took a place on the circle's edge, eyes closed, hands outstretched. I felt a surge of warmth, energy flowing through us, linking us together—a tangible bond of shared purpose.

However, within the harmonious connection, a cold shiver coursed through me. A sense of something watching us, lurking just beyond perception. Breaking the circle momentarily, I scanned our surroundings, but all seemed serene.

Clarissa caught my gaze, her eyes filled with understanding. "You felt it too?" she whispered.

I nodded, keeping my voice low so as not to alarm the others. "There's a presence here. We're not alone."

The realization hit us both simultaneously: the closer we drew to the Sanctum of Serenity, the more pronounced the shadows became. It was as if the dreamscape itself was testing our mettle, preparing us for the confrontation that was inevitably awaiting.

Lyria, ever perceptive, walked over. "We knew this journey wouldn't be without its dangers," , her voice firm yet gentle. "The sanctum is the dreamscape's heart, and it won't yield its secrets easily."

Adolwolf, having overheard our exchange, added, "The tome speaks of guardians—entities tasked with protecting the sanctum's purity. They are neither friend nor foe but test the intentions of those who seek entry."

As our preparations concluded and we set forth, tension pervaded. The dreamscape was no longer just a mesmerizing realm of wonders but a land fraught with challenges. Each step was measured, every sound scrutinized.

We began to ascend a silvery dune, its sands like fine crystal, reflecting the dreamscape's ethereal light. Reaching the crest, we beheld a sight of unparalleled splendor: a vast, shimmering lake, its surface mirror-smooth, with an island at its heart. The island radiated an otherworldly glow, and even from our distant vantage, it was clear—this was the entrance to the Sanctum of Serenity.

But between us and the island, the lake rippled with rarely seen geometric patterns, constantly shifting, altering, and forming maze-like pathways.

"This is our final trial," Elowen surmised, her gaze fixed on the island. "The Lake of Labyrinths. We must navigate its ever-changing paths to reach the sanctum."

Drawing a deep breath, I stepped forward, resolved to face whatever challenges lay ahead. "Together, we've come this far," I declared, addressing the group. "And together, we'll find our way through."

Their nods of agreement bolstered my spirits, and with renewed determination, we approached the lake's edge, ready to delve into the dreamscape's heart.

The water's edge lapped gently at our feet, its iridescent sheen reflecting all dreams and aspirations. Gazing into its depths, I could see images flicker: moments of joy, sorrow, love, and despair from countless souls. It was both beautiful and disconcerting.

Elowen dipped her fingers into the water, the liquid coiling around them like sentient tendrils. "The lake reacts to our thoughts and emotions," she observed. "We must tread with clear minds and focused intent."

Adolwolf, always our beacon of knowledge, nodded gravely. "Legends speak of those who wandered into the Lake of Labyrinths and became lost, their essences forever trapped within its mercurial depths. We must ensure our bond remains unbroken, for that is our best chance at navigating the maze."

Taking a deep breath, Clarissa stepped forward, her fingers clasping the delicate pendant hanging around her neck—a family heirloom passed down through generations. "I've always believed this held some power," she whispered, "a beacon in times of darkness. Let it guide us."

With Clarissa leading the way, the pendant casting a soft glow upon the waters, we formed a line, each of us placing a hand on the shoulder of the one in front. As we ventured onto the lake, the world around us began to shift. The dreamscape's ethereal light dimmed, replaced by a soft, luminescent blue that emanated from the water beneath our feet.

The lake's surface solidified into a tangible path, leading us deeper into the labyrinth. Walls of liquid rose on either side, their surfaces alive with fleeting images: a child's first laugh, a lover's embrace, the sting of betrayal, and the solace of redemption.

The weight of countless lives pressed in on us. I could hear distant echoes, whispers of memories long past. Every emotion, every fleeting thought of every dreamer who'd ever traversed this realm, was laid bare before us.

It was Lyria, with her unyielding spirit, who voiced the sentiment we all felt. "We must not get lost in these memories," she cautioned. "Remember, our own stories, our own dreams, are just as powerful."

Hours, or perhaps mere moments—it was hard to tell—passed as we wound our way through the ever-shifting maze. At times, the path broadened, offering glimpses of the island and the sanctum's ethereal glow. At other moments, it narrowed precariously, the dream walls closing in, threatening to envelop us.

It was during one of these narrow passages that the unexpected occurred. A shadowy figure emerged from the labyrinth's liquid walls, its form familiar, yet distorted. It was a reflection of me—or rather, a manifestation of my deepest fears and regrets.

"Rhineheart," it whispered, its voice a chilling echo of my own. "Why do you seek the sanctum? What do you hope to find? Redemption? Absolution?"

I stumbled back, mentally taken aback by the confrontation. The shadowy reflection continued, "You cannot escape who you are. The dreamscape knows all."

Lyria, her voice unwavering, stepped between me and the shadow. "We all have our past, our regrets," she declared. "But it's our ability to move forward, to grow and evolve, that defines us."

The shadowy apparition hesitated, its form wavering. Adolwolf, seizing the moment, began chanting verses from his tome. The ancient words resonated with power, causing the shadow to recoil.

With a final, defiant cry, it dissipated, leaving us shaken but resolute.

"We must remain vigilant," Elowen murmured. "The closer we get to the sanctum, the more intense the challenges will become."

Steadying myself, I nodded. "Let's move forward. Together."

With renewed determination, we pressed on, the Sanctum of Serenity beckoning us ever closer.

The path ahead began to bifurcate repeatedly, turning our linear journey into a decision-laden trial. Every divergence brought with it its own unique challenges, testing not just our resolve but the very fibers of our trust in one another. This dream-infused lake, with its labyrinthine detours, seemed to know the inner workings of our souls better than we did.

"I believe it's trying to tell us something," Elowen speculated, her gaze fixed on a particular junction that seemed to shimmer more brightly than the others. "It might not be just about reaching the sanctum, but about the lessons we learn along the way."

Clarissa, pragmatic, responded, "Or it might just be doing everything in its power to prevent us from reaching our destination. The dreamscape is not without its guardians or defenses."

As if on cue, a deep humming filled the air, a resonating frequency that caused the waters to ripple and our bones to vibrate sympathetically. From the previously tranquil waters, shadows began to emerge, melding and weaving together to form ephemeral, spectral figures.

"We've stirred the protectors of this realm," Lyria muttered, drawing a short, luminous blade from her side.

Adolwolf's fingers skimmed the pages of his tome, searching for a spell or incantation that might shield us. "Stay close," he advised.

I felt a magnetic pull from one of the branching paths, an inexplicable connection, almost as if the path itself was summoning me. "This way," I announced, trying to sound more confident than I felt. The spectral guardians, noticing our decision, glided ominously in our direction, their forms becoming more defined, their intentions clear.

As we hurried along the chosen pathway, I could feel the collective memories of the lake intertwining with my own, the recollections of countless dreamers merging with my narrative. Their hopes, fears, loves, and losses added layers of depth to my perception, painting our current endeavor in richer hues of meaning.

Our sprint became a marathon as the path led us on a meandering course, twisting and turning in ways that defied logic. The phantasmal guardians were relentless in their pursuit, their ghostly wails echoing with both longing and rage.

A sudden clearing appeared before us, revealing an ethereal bridge made of luminous strands of light. It spanned a vast expanse of the dream-lake, connecting our current pathway to a distant isle bathed in a gentle glow. On its shores stood the imposing facade of the Shadow Sanctum, concealing that of the Sanctum Of Serenity.

"We need to cross!" Elowen exclaimed. But as we approached, the guardians converged, attempting to sever the strands of the bridge.

Adolwolf, mustering his strength, began a chant that sounded ancient, even primal. The words formed a protective barrier around us, allowing us to step onto the bridge. The ethereal strands held firm under our weight, pulsing with an energy that seemed to resonate with our collective heartbeat.

Lyria, with her blade drawn, fended off the closest shadows, ensuring our passage remained unimpeded. Each slash sent ripples through the dream realm, creating momentary disturbances that slowed the guardians.

But just as victory seemed within grasp, a larger, more formidable shadow emerged from the lake's depths. This guardian was different, its presence emanating power and authority. It hovered at the bridge's end, blocking our path to the sanctum.

The journey to reclaim what was lost, it seemed, was far from over.

Each step we took towards the looming shadow felt heavier, as if the very air around us was forming a gravitational pull, becoming a viscous substance trying to deter our advance. The lake's luminosity, which had once seemed comforting, now cast eerie patterns on the bridge, reflecting off the translucent shapes of our ethereal adversaries.

Clarissa, with newfound determination burning in her eyes, spoke softly, her voice weaving a melody that seemed ancient yet familiar. The notes rippled across the bridge, causing the spectral guardians to momentarily falter. But the colossal guardian at the end remained unaffected, its immense form a testament to its dominion over this dream-bound realm.

Elowen, drawing from the wellspring of her intuition, whispered, "This guardian is not just a protector; it's an embodiment of the trials and tribulations faced by those who ventured here before us. It's an amalgamation of their fears, regrets, and unfulfilled desires."

It dawned on me that to truly move past this obstacle, we'd need more than physical prowess or magical aptitude. This was a challenge that called for introspection, a confrontation with our innermost demons.

As if hearing my thoughts, Lyria approached the guardian, her luminous blade still in hand. "If you are a manifestation of the memories and emotions of dreamers, then perhaps you can be reasoned with," she asserted, her voice carrying a cadence of both authority and compassion.

The guardian responded, not with words but with images, conjuring visions of dreams past. We saw fleeting moments of joy, elongated stretches of sorrow, and everything in between. It was another reminder of the transitory nature of existence and the transformative emotions that define the human experience.

Adolwolf, our scholar, seemed to decipher a pattern in the chaos. "These memories," he voiced aloud, "they aren't just random. There's a narrative, a sequence. If we can understand it, perhaps we can appeal to this guardian's better nature."

For what felt like hours, we delved into the cascade of emotions and memories, trying to discern the underlying story. We shared our insights, pieced together fragments, and slowly began to understand the essence of the guardian's existence.

It was a tale of love and loss, of dreams achieved and dreams shattered, of enduring friendships and bitter betrayals. In many ways, it mirrored our own journey, reminding us of the legacy we hoped to leave behind.

Emboldened by our revelations, I took a step forward. "We acknowledge your purpose, guardian," I began, my voice echoing across the dreamscape. "But we also recognize our shared humanity, our shared dreams. Let us pass, not as intruders, but as fellow dreamers seeking to understand and be understood."

A tense silence ensued, during which the guardian seemed to contemplate our plea. And then, with a sound like a sigh, it began to dissipate, breaking apart into countless luminous fragments that rejoined the shimmering lake.

We crossed the bridge, the entrance to the Shadow Sanctum now open yet unwelcoming. But as we ventured forward, I couldn't help but reflect on the guardian's legacy. It had imparted to us an invaluable lesson about the interconnectedness of dreams and the universality of human experience. And as we moved closer to our goal, that lesson would serve as a guiding light, illuminating our path and our purpose.

The Shadow Sanctum, unlike how we first remembered it, portrayed itself now contrary to its name. Instead, it was a sprawling complex of crystalline structures that refracted light in mesmerizing patterns. The ground beneath our feet felt like a living entity, pulsating with a rhythm that mirrored the heartbeat of the dreamscape.

We ventured further in, guided by the labyrinthine layout of the Sanctum. Murmurs echoed from distant corners – whispers of dreams long lost, seeking an audience, perhaps a momentary resurgence.

"Every dream that has ever been dreamt resides here," Lyria whispered, her fingers gently caressing a nearby crystal. The moment she touched it, the crystal pulsed, projecting a series of vivid images. There were scenes of children playing under golden suns, lovers sharing secret glances under the canopy of starlit nights, and warriors bravely facing formidable adversaries.

Releasing the crystal, she turned to us, her eyes gleaming with newfound understanding. "The dreams here are alive, waiting for someone to experience them again, if only for a fleeting moment."

Elowen, her senses always attuned to the intricacies of the dreamscape, nodded in agreement. "We're not just here to reclaim Clarissa's shadow. We're treading a path that countless others have journeyed before us. Their memories, aspirations, and deepest fears are interwoven into the very fabric of this realm."

Adolwolf, who had been silently observing a particularly luminescent crystal, spoke up, "It's not just about finding Clarissa's shadow. It's about understanding the delicate balance of dreams and reality. Our experiences here could profoundly shape our understanding of the waking world."

Clarissa, her face a palette of hope and certainty, added, "And perhaps, in understanding the essence of this realm, I can come to terms with the fragmented parts of myself. Reclaiming my shadow isn't just a physical act; it's a journey of self-realization."

We moved deeper into the Sanctum, with each step unveiling more layers of the dreamscape's intricate tapestry. Occasionally, one of us would be drawn to a particular crystal, momentarily experiencing a dream that resonated with our own desires or fears.

It was during one such moment that I came across a crystal that seemed eerily familiar. As I reached out to touch it, a torrent of memories engulfed me. I saw scenes from my childhood, my family, and moments of profound joy and heartbreaking sorrow. But among these memories was one that stood out – a dream where I had met a young girl with fiery red hair, a spirit as untamed as the winds.

Elowen.

The realization hit me with the force of a tidal wave. We had met in a dream, long before our paths crossed in the waking world. The intricate dance of fate and destiny had intertwined our lives in ways we couldn't fathom.

Pulling away from the crystal, I sought Elowen's gaze. Her eyes, wide with astonishment, confirmed what I already knew. Our connection ran deeper than mere camaraderie. We were bound by the ephemeral threads of dreams, a bond that transcended the boundaries of time and space. With this newfound understanding, our resolve strengthened.

Chapter 11: Resonance of Dreams

The Shadow Sanctum's vastness seemed to stretch beyond the horizon, its crystalline spires soaring towards the heavens, capturing and refracting dreams of both the living and the departed. Each shimmering structure told stories of millennia, memories carved by dreamers who had lost and reclaimed parts of themselves here.

As we traversed deeper into this realm, the dreams grew more potent, more personal. Elowen and I shared stolen glances, our previously undisclosed connection in the dreamscape now forming an unspoken bond between us. Yet, this bond had its complexities – for how does one navigate a relationship built on the ever-shifting sands of dreams?

Adolwolf, perhaps sensing our silent struggle, began to share tales of dreamers he'd encountered in his long years as a guardian of the dreamscape. "Not all connections formed in dreams translate seamlessly into reality," he intoned. "The dreamscape is a realm of unbridled emotions and desires. What seems profound here might not hold the same weight in the waking world."

Lyria, countered, "But isn't the intensity of emotion what makes dreams so powerful? The rawness, the vulnerability – these are what make dreams resonate deeply within us."

Adolwolf chuckled, "And that's the eternal struggle, isn't it? Balancing the profound depth of dreams with the pragmatic reality of waking life."

While their discourse added layers of depth to our journey, Clarissa's mission remained our central focus. As we neared the heart of the Sanctum, the dreams around us grew denser, their narratives more convoluted. The Shadows Sanctums Serenity Core, where Clarissa's shadow was believed to be held, was the epicenter of it all.

A massive obsidian structure stood at the very heart of the Sanctum. It was the antithesis of everything around it – absorbing light rather than refracting it. Its surface pulsed with a dark energy that was draining, even from a distance. Clarissa hesitated, her steps faltering as we approached.

"It's okay, Clarissa," Lyria whispered, taking her hand. "Remember, your shadow is a part of you, an echo of your soul. We're here to help you reclaim it."

The entrance to the Shadow Core beckoned, a portal of swirling darkness. As we stepped into its depths, we were immediately enveloped in an almost stifling silence. The dreams here were not vivid or vibrant but rather subdued, mere whispers of their former selves.

Navigating this space was akin to wading through a thick fog, where shadows – both lost and reclaimed – danced just out of reach. Clarissa, drawing strength from our presence, began to call out to her shadow, her voice echoing through the cavernous expanse.

And then, from the depths of the darkness, a familiar silhouette began to emerge. Clarissa's shadow, fragmented and forlorn, slowly made its way towards us. As it neared, however, it became evident that reclaiming it wouldn't be as simple as we had hoped.

Bound to her shadow were countless other strands of darkness, each representing a dream or memory Clarissa had lost in her journey. To truly reclaim her shadow, Clarissa would need to confront and untangle each of these strands, reliving moments of pain, joy, love, and loss.

The challenge was daunting, but with our combined strength and resolve, we began the intricate process of unraveling Clarissa's past. Each memory confronted brought with it a rush of emotion, a vivid snapshot of a life lived in both the waking world and the dreamscape.

And as we delved deeper, it became clear that Clarissa's journey was not just about reclaiming a lost part of herself but also about understanding the complex tapestry of her life and the dreams that had shaped it. The Shadow Sanctum, in all its enigmatic glory, was but a mirror reflecting the multifaceted nature of our very souls.

With every memory that Clarissa reclaimed, the weight of her past pressed against her, at times almost unbearably. Tears streamed down her face as forgotten memories played out before us: a young Clarissa laughing with her mother beneath the sun, an adolescent Clarissa tasting the bitterness of her first heartbreak, a more recent memory of standing at the precipice of a decision that would alter her life's trajectory.

"These memories," she murmured, her voice laden with emotion, "I had locked them away, too scared to face them."

Elowen reached out, gently wiping away Clarissa's tears. "Dreams and memories are intertwined, my dear. What we experience in our waking lives influences the worlds we create in our slumber. And sometimes, to protect ourselves, we push away the most painful memories, even if it means sacrificing a part of our soul."

Clarissa nodded, taking a shaky breath. "But I'm ready now. Ready to face them all."

I admired her courage, the raw determination she displayed in the face of her tumultuous past. As a guide, it was my role to support her, and as her memories unfurled, I couldn't help but feel a surge of protectiveness. Yet, it wasn't just my duty to guide her; our past encounters, veiled in the mists of shared dreams, forged a connection deeper than either of us had realized.

With each memory that Clarissa confronted, the Shadow Core's oppressive atmosphere began to wane. The darkness that had once consumed the space now receded, replaced by a luminescent glow that seemed to emanate from Clarissa herself. It was a physical representation of her inner transformation, a beacon of hope in a realm of shadows.

As the final strands of darkness were untangled and Clarissa's shadow merged back into her, the transformation of the Shadow Core was complete. The obsidian structure now pulsed with a gentle, golden light, its once foreboding presence transformed into a symbol of hope and rebirth.

Adolwolf, at times a stoic guardian, looked on with a rare smile gracing his lips. "You've done it, Clarissa. You've not only reclaimed your shadow but also illuminated the heart of the Sanctum."

Clarissa, her eyes shimmering with unshed tears, whispered, "I couldn't have done it without all of you."

Lyria, wrapping an arm around her, replied, "We're a team, bound by dreams and destiny. Always remember that."

As we made our way out of the Shadow Core, the entire Sanctum seemed to come alive, resonating with the triumphant energy of Clarissa's victory. The crystalline spires sung a harmonious tune, a celestial lullaby that whispered promises of hope and new beginnings.

However, even amidst the jubilation, I felt a tinge of unease. The Sanctum, for all its mysteries, held secrets even deeper than the Shadow Core. And as we journeyed on, I couldn't shake off the feeling that our challenges were far from over.

The crystalline spires stood tall, like sentinels of old, echoing tales from times when dreamers were plentiful and the boundaries between the real and the ethereal were more porous. These were times when humanity held its dreams in the highest regard, understanding their ability to shape realities and forge destinies. Now, however, it seemed the art of dreaming had been relegated to the confines of nighttime musings, forgotten by daybreak.

The Sanctums core was more than just a repository of dreams; it was a haven, a space where memories and aspirations intertwined, creating tapestries of potent emotions and desires. Yet, with Clarissa's reclamation of her shadow, a new energy pulsated throughout, an energy that was both invigorating and perturbing.

"We should be cautious," Elowen whispered, her eyes scanning the vastness of the Sanctum. "The harmonization of the Shadow Core has undoubtedly sent ripples throughout this realm. Forces that were dormant may now stir."

Adolwolf nodded in agreement. "I've traversed the Sanctum countless times, but the aura today feels... different. We need to tread lightly."

Clarissa clutched the pendant around her neck, the gem pulsing in rhythm with her heartbeat. "This place," she murmured, "it feels alive, almost sentient. Like it's observing us, waiting."

Lyria, with feelings of optimism, voiced, "It's as if the Sanctum itself is breathing, its every exhale a sigh of relief, and its inhale drawing in our hopes and fears."

I felt the subtle undercurrents of the Sanctum's energies, and deep within, a connection stirred—a connection I had long buried. Memories of shared dreams with Elowen, the mingling of our consciousness in realms untethered by reality, surged forth. This place was a reflection of those dreams, a physical manifestation of the abstract.

"We should keep moving," I suggested, eager to escape the weight of my reminiscence. "The heart of the Sanctum awaits, and with it, perhaps, answers to the questions that plague us."

As we ventured deeper, the crystalline pathways shifted, almost organically, creating a circular spiral of shimmering corridors. The very walls seemed to breathe, their surfaces undulating softly, as if caressed by an unseen wind. The sound— a mellifluous hum— resonated with our very souls, an otherworldly lullaby that beckoned us further into the heart of the enigma.

The Sanctum's essence was intertwined with the dreams of countless beings, and as we moved, snippets of these dreams flitted around us. A child's innocent amusement, the whispered promises of lovers, the sorrowful sighs of the heartbroken, and the hopeful gaze of dreamers yearning for more.

Yet, amidst the beauty and wonder, a dissonance emerged. An undercurrent of darkness, an energy that seemed out of place. And as it grew more pronounced, a realization dawned upon us: the Sanctum was not just a guardian of dreams. It held nightmares too, and they were beginning to stir.

The juxtaposition of dreams and nightmares within the Sanctum created an ambience of conflicting energies. Warm hues of golden dreams clashed with the cold, ethereal blues of the nightmares, casting fragmented, kaleidoscopic patterns on the crystalline walls. These contrasts only intensified as we approached the heart of the Sanctum.

Clarissa paused, her breath catching. "Can you feel it? The intensity of emotions, the raw power that courses through this place. It's overwhelming."

Adolwolf gently touched a nearby crystal. "This isn't just a place of dormant energies. These dreams and nightmares are very much alive, reacting, evolving, sometimes even fighting for dominance."

Lyria's sharp gaze caught something in the distance. "Look," she whispered, pointing. A swirling vortex of inky blackness loomed, casting ominous shadows and exuding an energy that felt cold and alien. "That is where we must go. The Heart of the Sanctum of Serenity and the source of the disharmony."

Elowen looked troubled, her face pale under the surreal lighting. "When dreams and nightmares coalesce, they can birth entities. These entities can be benign or malevolent, shaped by the very emotions that birthed them."

I felt a tug in the pit of my stomach, an instinctual warning. "Then we should be prepared for whatever awaits. If what Elowen says is true, we could face something beyond our comprehension."

A symphony of whispered voices, both melodic and discordant, surrounded us as we ventured closer to the vortex. Each step seemed heavier than the last, and the ambient glow diminished, plunging us into an ever-deepening twilight.

Suddenly, Clarissa's pendant flared with a brilliant light, illuminating the path ahead. "It's guiding us," she murmured. "Or warning us."

From the vortex's core, tentacles of anti-matter made of the darkest of darkness began to snake out, reaching for us. But they recoiled upon touching the light emanating from Clarissa's pendant. The Heart of the Sanctum sensed our approach and wasn't passive in its reception.

Adolwolf, chanting a meditation of the crown chakra, created an otherworldly blade of light, with a protective glow, it pulsated an orb around us. "Stay close," he advised. "Whatever resides within that vortex might not appreciate our intrusion."

The intensity of the emotions swirling around us became a burden. Hope, fear, love, despair, joy, sorrow — the unending feelings of countless souls seemed to cry out, yearning to be acknowledged, to be felt.

As we stood at the precipice, ready to face the Heart of the Sanctum and the unknown entity birthed from the confluence of dreams and nightmares, I couldn't help but ponder: Were we here to restore harmony, or would our presence only amplify the chaos? What awaited us within that vortex, and more importantly, would we emerge unchanged?

TEROA

Within moments of that reflection, a surge of energy enveloped us. The ground beneath seemed to tremble, and the very air grew thick, charged with expectation. The vortex, once a distant menace, now seemed to loom even larger, pulsating with a life of its own.

Lyria, whose vast knowledge of the arcane often provided insight, murmured, "it's an electromagnetic gravitational convergence point. A place where all dreams and nightmares meet, clash, and sometimes, meld."

Elowen took a step forward, her eyes fixed on the swirling chaos. "The boundaries here are thin. Not just between dreams and nightmares, but between this world and others. We tread a fragile path."

Suddenly, a voice, ethereal yet resonant, echoed through the Sanctum. "Why have you come? Seekers of light in a realm of shadows?"

It wasn't a singular voice, but a cacophony — layers of whispers and cries, joy and sorrow, hope and despair. Clarissa clutched her pendant tighter. "We've come to restore balance, to reclaim that which has been lost. We seek understanding."

The voices laughed, a haunting melody that echoed throughout the crystalline caverns. "Balance? In a place of eternal flux? Such is the folly of mortals. But your quest intrigues us. Step forth into the vortex, if you dare, and behold the truth."

With a shared, determined nod, we began our passage into the vortex. The world around shifted, the once sharp lines of the Sanctum blurring, melding into a canvas of ever-changing colors and forms. My senses were overwhelmed; I felt both weightless and burdened, cold yet burning, lost but also profoundly found.

As the world settled, we found ourselves in an expansive chamber, the ceiling lost to an endless expanse of stars, each twinkling with its own rhythm. At the chamber's center stood a colossal figure, formed from shimmering motes of light and shadow. It was neither solid nor transparent, constantly shifting between forms — now a mighty beast, then a delicate bird, and next a towering tree.

"This is The Nexus," whispered Lyria, awe evident in her voice. "The embodiment of the Sanctum's power."

The Nexus shifted its gaze to each of us, its eyes— if one could call them that— a swirling mix of constellations. "Seekers," it began, its voice now singular, calm, and deep. "You stand at the crossroads of creation and annihilation, hope and despair. What hope do you bring to tip the balance?"

It was a challenge, a plea, and a question all in one. And as I met its gaze, memories of our journey, our purpose, and the legacy we hoped to leave behind surged forth. The answer, I felt, would shape not just our fate but that of the Sanctum and all who dwelt within its shimmering walls. And in that moment a shift occurred and we rose what felt like a thousand light years straight into the staring constellations above, only to appear before a path never traveled, still within the Sanctum.

Chapter 12: Veil of the Shadows

The path before us was paved with purple light, a shimmering guide through the inky darkness of the newly familiar Sanctum. The deeper we ventured, the more the atmosphere grew charged, almost sentient. Wisps of memory and echoes of dreams danced around us, intertwining with our thoughts and making it hard to discern where one's own recollections ended and another's began.

Clarissa, her hand resting on the pendant around her neck, whispered, "It feels like walking through a never before dreamt dream, feeling forever timeless. Every step we take echoes back ages and reverberates into futures yet unknown."

Elowen nodded in agreement. "It's a conduit of time and emotion, of desires, ambitions, fears, and memories."

Adolwolf, typically stoic, frowned. "How do we maintain our purpose, our individuality, in a place designed to blend the boundaries of self?"

"We stay close," I answered, looking around at the team I had come to view as family. "We lean on each other. The Sanctum might blur the edges of our identity, but together, our combined strength and determination will see us through."

The path gradually widened, revealing a vast chamber bathed in a kaleidoscope of hues. In the center stood an imposingly familiar obsidian dais, atop which rested a crystal so brilliantly luminous that it was painful to look at directly.

"This... this is the heart," Elowen murmured, her voice tinged with reverence. And, as I hope you haven't forgotten, where we shall learn the Song of Veils.

"Song of Veils?" Lyria questioned. "Is this is the elusive song we have been looking for all along?"

This is where we would learn that great and wondrous song that would provide a means to counter imbalances in the dream world.

As we approached, the crystal's glow intensified, revealing the silhouettes of countless figures trapped within — shadows, memories, dreams. All merged, yearning to break free.

Clarissa hesitated, her usually fierce demeanor replaced by a look of vulnerability. "I can feel it... part of my shadow is in there! But how do we set it free without releasing everything else?"

Before anyone could respond, a voice, both ancient and timeless, echoed throughout the chamber. "Seekers of balance, you stand at the precipice of choice. One cannot reclaim without sacrifice. What are you willing to offer in exchange for the shadow's freedom? And the Song of all Songs that you seek?"

Elowen, her face pale but resolute, replied, "Our intentions are pure. We seek only to restore what was taken, to mend the balance. If memories are the currency of this place, then take mine. All my experiences, good and bad, in exchange for Clarissa's shadowy fragment."

The crystal pulsed, almost as if considering the offer. "Memories alone won't suffice. It requires emotion, raw and unfiltered. Joy, pain, love, fear — the very essence of humanity."

I stepped forward, taking Elowen's hand. "Then take from all of us. Our collective experiences, emotions, everything that makes us human. But let Clarissa be whole again. And release the Song of Songs"

The chamber filled with a deafening silence, the weight of our decision pressing heavily upon us. And then, in a rush of wind and light, the crystal shattered, releasing the shadows, memories, and melodies within. The room was awash with color and emotion, but in the midst of the chaos, Clarissa's shadow gracefully merged with her, making her complete once more, as an otherworldly melody filled the air.

As the tempest subsided, the voice returned, now softer, almost tender. "Balance has been restored, but at a cost. Your memories remain, but the intensity of your emotions has been dimmed. Protect this balance, for the Sanctum's equilibrium depends on it. The Song of Songs could not have been released without first captivating Clarissa's shadow. The Song of Songs contains melodies and harmonies that represent all of you, and thus all of humanity. The song resides within each of you, and will be understood fully when the time requires it."

The journey had taken its toll, but we had succeeded. As we made our way out of the Sanctum, our bond stronger than ever, I couldn't help but wonder about the price we had paid. Were our emotions truly diminished, or had the Sanctum simply taken the extremes, leaving us more centered, more balanced?

Time would tell.

As we retraced our steps through the winding paths of the Sanctum, the world around us seemed altered, yet eerily familiar. Every shadow we passed whispered of tales forgotten, of dreams that once were, and of a future not yet realized.

The absence of extremes in our emotions became more evident with every step. I looked at Clarissa, her face radiant in her wholeness, yet the fierce fire that once burned in her eyes was replaced with a gentle glow. A sacrifice, yes, but she looked at peace. She caught my gaze and gave me a soft, understanding smile.

Elowen moved gracefully beside me, her once vivacious spirit now possessing a calming serenity. "Do you regret it, Rhineheart?" she asked, her voice soft.

I thought for a moment. "Regret is a strong emotion, and like all others, it feels... distant now. I did what felt right. For Clarissa, for all of us. Do you?"

She hesitated, then sighed, "There's a tranquility in this new state of being. But already, in the fleeting shadows of my thoughts, I do yearn for the highs and lows that once defined us. However, I believe our sacrifice has granted us a unique perspective, one that not many possess."

As we approached the exit of the Sanctum, Adolwolf, usually a man of few words, paused and addressed the group. "We've been changed by this place, by our choices. It's essential that we remember the reason behind our sacrifice. We did it for balance, unity, and for each other. Our emotions might be tempered, but our bond remains unbreakable."

Outside, the real world awaited. With our newfound serenity, tasks that once seemed insurmountable now appeared achievable. Our journey had reshaped us, but our purpose remained intact.

The four of us, bound by our shared experience, found solace in each other's company. We established a haven, a place where those affected by the whims of the Sanctum could find respite and understanding.

Our story spread, and many came to seek our guidance. They brought tales of lost shadows, stolen dreams, and the hope of finding balance. In guiding them, we discovered a new purpose, and in doing so, our legacy was forged.

Yet, in the quiet moments, when the world's noise faded, I couldn't help but ponder the voice's final words in the Sanctum. Had we truly achieved equilibrium? Or was there still a deeper balance to be found?

As the sun set, casting a golden hue over our haven, I realized that our journey was yet still, even with all of its revelations, far from over. The Sanctum had given us a purpose, but it was up to us to determine our destiny. And as the night descended, our next dreams awaited.

Over time I noticed the nights were different now. I would lie down, and instead of the tumultuous dreams that once plagued me, there was a calm vastness. It was as if I was floating in an infinite sea of light, where time and space lost their meaning. Yet, even in this expanse, I felt a constant pull, a gentle tug directing me to something, or someone.

One such evening, as I lay in this dreamlike state, a form began to emerge from the mists of my consciousness. It was a tree, grand in its stature, its leaves shimmering silver in the moonlight, roots plunging deep into the heart of the earth. Beneath its shade stood a figure, one I recognized immediately despite never having met her in this realm.

It was Morphean.

"Rhineheart," his voice echoed, sounding both distant and near. "You've journeyed far, yet your path is still unfolding."

I approached him, noting the ethereal quality of his presence. "Morphean, why are we meeting here?"

"This is the place between dreams and reality," he explained, his eyes reflecting the stars above. "Our souls resonate on a frequency that allows us to connect in this dimension."

I looked around, taking in the serene beauty. "Why have you brought me here?"

"To remind you," he boomed, his gaze directed towards the stars. "The Sanctum of Serentiy was just the beginning. Your true purpose, the essence of your legacy, is still waiting to be unearthed. The balance you seek is not just within, but in the world around you."

I felt a rush of memories, flashes of our time in the Sanctum, the sacrifices, the lessons. "How do we achieve this balance?"

He stepped closer, placing a hand over my heart. "You must first understand the nature of shadows. They are not just absences of light but are entities of their own. To truly find balance, one must embrace both light and shadow."

I pondered his words, recalling the experience of merging with my shadow side. "But we've been through this, haven't we? In the Sanctum."

Morphean smiled, a confidence present in his expression. "That was but a taste, a glimpse. There's more, Rhineheart. Much more. And it's not just about personal balance, but the balance of the world."

A gust of wind rustled the leaves, and I felt a shiver run down my spine. "What must we do?"

He looked up, his gaze distant. "A great imbalance approaches, a force that threatens to plunge the world into eternal darkness. You and the others are destined to stand against it. But to succeed, you must seek out the ancient guardians of balance, learn their secrets, and bring together the light and the shadow."

The weight of hiswords bore down on me, but there was also a newfound determination. "We'll face it, whatever it is. Together."

Morphean nodded, his form starting to fade. "Remember, Rhineheart, in shadows lie not just fear but also the answers. Seek them out."

As he disappeared, the tree and the dreamlike landscape dissolved, leaving me floating in the vast sea of light once more. When I awoke, the first rays of dawn were breaking...

I rose from the comfort of the bed in our dream haven, feeling the remnants of the dream cling to me. The air in the room was electric, as though the very walls knew that our journey was taking a momentous turn.

At the ground levels of the haven within the realm of Ashcrofts Estate, I found Clarissa seated at the dining table, sipping on a cup of tea. She looked up as I entered, her eyes searching mine. "Another dream?" she inquired, noting the contemplative expression on my face.

I nodded, recounting the encounter with Morphean. As the details flowed, I could see the weight of the revelation settling on Clarissa. When I finished, she looked out of the window for a few moments, processing the implications.

"We always knew this was bigger than us," she finally said, turning back to me, her gaze resolute. "If there are ancient guardians who can help us, then we need to find them."

We both knew that the task ahead wouldn't be simple. Locating beings of legend, especially in a world teeming with myth and magic, was like searching for a single star in the vast night sky. Still, there was a glimmer of hope; our connection to the realm of dreams could be the key.

As the day progressed, we gathered the others. Adolwolf, with his vast knowledge of lore, Elowen, with her uncanny ability to decipher mysteries, and Lyria, our bridge between realms. Together, we began pouring over ancient texts, maps, and scrolls, seeking any clue about the guardians of balance.

Hours turned into days as we submerged ourselves in the lore of the world. One evening, while everyone else was taking a break, I stumbled upon a tattered journal. It was penned by a dreamwalker, like us, who spoke of his encounters with ethereal beings that guarded the balance of the world. His descriptions resonated with Morphean's words.

The dreamwalker wrote of a hidden sanctuary, nestled deep within the Forest of Perception. It was said to be the dwelling place of the first guardian, a being who could control the essence of light itself.

The journal also mentioned trials, challenges set by the guardians to test the worth of those who sought them out. It was clear that our journey would not just be about finding these guardians but proving ourselves worthy of their knowledge.

"This could be our first lead," I declared, sharing the journal's contents with the others. There was a spark of excitement, a sense of purpose that had been missing for a while. We would venture into the forest in search of the first guardian.

However, as we prepared for our expedition, a sense of unease settled over me. The realm of dreams had offered guidance and insights, but it had also shown us the magnitude of the challenge ahead. Balancing light and shadow were no simple task, and as the weight of our responsibility grew, so did the shadows that lurked in the corners of my mind.

The Forest of Perception, as the tales had painted it, was an ever-shifting corridor of ancient trees, verdant undergrowth, and secrets whispered by the wind. But the tales had also mentioned its beauty, an ethereal shimmer that seemed to paint every leaf and twig, every blade of grass and petal. It was as if the forest itself breathed magic.

However, no tale had prepared me for the tangible pulse of life that emanated from every part of the forest. As our party ventured deeper into its heart, it felt as though the trees whispered stories of old, echoing memories of all who'd tread these paths before.

Elowen, always attuned to the rhythms of nature, often stopped to touch a tree trunk or listen to a brook. "This forest," she remarked, her eyes distant, "remembers everything. Every footstep, every whisper. It's a living, breathing chronicle."

Adolwolf, on the other hand, was lost in the scribbles of his journal, constantly jotting down notes and sketching the peculiar flora and fauna we encountered. At one point, he paused to marvel at a luminous mushroom, its glow illuminating the pages of his book.

"We're not alone," Lyria whispered as we set up camp one evening. I followed her gaze to see shadows flitting between the trees, their forms insubstantial and wraith-like. They seemed to be observing us, their intentions unclear.

Night in the forest was unlike any other. The very canopy seemed alight with a million stars, while the forest floor shimmered with bioluminescent plants and creatures. But it was also alive with sounds - distant calls, rustling leaves, and the soft, harmonious hum of nature.

It was during one such night that she appeared. Emerging from a curtain of iridescent mist was a figure draped in robes of shimmering white, her very being radiating an otherworldly glow. Her hair, cascading down like a river of moonlight, framed a face of ageless beauty. She moved with a grace that seemed to defy the laws of the physical realm, each step as fluid and gentle as a falling leaf.

"I am Lysandra," her voice echoed, soft and melodic, yet carrying the weight of ages. "Guardian of the First Light. You seek balance, dreamwalkers, but balance comes at a price."

I stepped forward, the weight of our mission pushing me to speak, "We are prepared to pay any price, Guardian. The balance of our world, and the very essence of dreams, is at stake."

She regarded me with eyes that seemed to pierce my very soul. "Very well," she responded, her tone enigmatic. "But remember, dreamwalker, balance is not always what it seems. Light and shadow, they are but two sides of the same coin. To truly understand balance, you must embrace both."

With those words, Lysandra beckoned us to follow her. As we ventured deeper into the heart of the forest, I couldn't help but wonder what trials lay ahead and whether we were truly prepared for the challenges the guardians would set before us. The weight of Lysandra's words echoed in my mind, and I hoped, fervently, that we would find the answers we sought.

The path Lysandra led us on twisted and meandered through the forest, often so subtly that the surroundings seemed unchanged. But with each step, a sense of growing anticipation hung in the air. The forest sensed our journey, and in some inexplicable way, was molding itself in response.

It wasn't long before we reached a clearing bathed in silver moonlight. Here, an ancient stone circle stood, the monoliths bearing cryptic engravings eroded by time. The very ground seemed to thrum with energy, a vibration that resonated through our bones.

Lysandra stepped into the center of the circle and gestured for us to follow. We did, forming a smaller circle within the stones. The air grew dense yet uplifting, charged with an electrifying anticipation.

"Dreamwalkers," Lysandra began, her voice carrying an ethereal quality that made it seem as though it came from both everywhere and nowhere, "you've come seeking balance, but first, you must face the imbalances within yourselves."

As she spoke, shadows detached from the monoliths and danced around us. They weren't threatening but bore the visages of our pasts, memories, regrets, dreams unfulfilled, and moments of self-doubt. I saw myself, younger, reckless, making choices I'd come to regret. It was a visceral reminder of the internal battles I had faced, some of which still raged.

Beside me, Lyria seemed to be confronting her own phantoms, her usually bright eyes clouded with pain. Elowen's face was a canvas of sorrow as she reached out to a shadow that bore the likeness of a young child. Adolwolf's face was a mask, but the rapid scribbling in his journal was more frantic than I'd ever seen.

"These are the parts of you that you've hidden, ignored, or wished away," Lysandra continued. "To restore balance, you must first acknowledge and accept them."

Each shadow approached its counterpart, and a cold chill swept over me as mine drew near. But instead of fear, a sense of understanding bloomed. This shadow wasn't an enemy; it was a part of me. I reached out, and as our fingers touched, a rush of memories flooded through me—lessons learned, wounds that had shaped me, and strength forged in adversity.

One by one, as we faced and embraced our shadows, they melded back into us. The air grew lighter, the oppressive weight lifting. Lysandra nodded approvingly. "Balance begins within. And now, your true journey commences."

The forest around us shifted, and a previously unseen path revealed itself, leading deeper into the unknown. But there was no fear in our steps now. The trials of the Enchanted Forest had only just begun, but in confronting our internal struggles, we had taken the most crucial step forward.

And as we journeyed onward, I couldn't shake off a feeling—an intuition—that Lysandra's words bore deeper meanings than we'd perceived. What lay ahead was more than a mere quest for balance; it was a journey into the very essence of existence.

The path that unfolded before us seemed to lead straight into the mind of the forest. The canopy overhead became denser, the foliage a deeper shade of green, and the very atmosphere carried a moist, earthy aroma that was both invigorating and mysterious.

A part of me longed to see the sky, to glimpse a reassuring hint of blue above, but it remained hidden, shrouded by the interlocking branches. The forest was both protector and prison. It was easy to lose one's sense of direction here. But Lysandra moved with a purpose, her steps deliberate, as if the very trees whispered their secrets to her.

Elowen, still visibly affected by her encounter with the shadow of the child, walked alongside Adolwolf. Every now and then, I would hear a soft murmur from Adolwolf, reading out verses from his journal, attempting to console and ground her.

Lyria, on the other hand, seemed more curious than fearful. She reached out occasionally, touching the unique flora, sometimes plucking a leaf or flower, studying it intently, then carefully storing it in her pouch. I recalled her mentioning her apothecary training, and how she believed that every plant held a purpose, a remedy for some ailment.

Walking alongside her, I ventured, "Do you think there's a plant here that might help us in our quest?"

Lyria looked up, her eyes thoughtful. "Every environment provides for its inhabitants. The Forest of Perception is no different. We just need to understand its language." She held up a blue-tinged leaf. "This, for example, can induce deep, dreamless sleep, useful if one needs to rest without the interruptions of dreams."

I nodded, intrigued. "We might need that, considering where we are."

We continued on, the forest around us alive with sounds—distant bird calls, the rustling of unseen creatures, the whispering of leaves. The path began to slope gently downwards, leading us into what felt like a valley. A thin mist began to gather, gradually thickening with every step, reducing visibility. Soon, it was like walking through a white void, the only indication of a path being the feel of trodden earth beneath our feet.

Suddenly, Lysandra halted. Through the dense fog, a faint blue glow emanated ahead. As we squinted through the haze, the outline of a vast, shimmering lake came into view, its waters aglow with phosphorescence. On its edge stood an ancient willow tree, its branches drooping into the water, every leaf glowing with a soft luminescence.

Lysandra turned to us, her voice low. "The Luminous Lake," she whispered. "It is said that its waters can show one their destiny, but its truths are not for the faint of heart."

I could feel the weight of her words. It was a crossroads of sorts, another test, perhaps even more challenging than the shadows. The waters beckoned, but did I have the courage to face whatever they might reveal?

With a deep breath, I stepped towards the lake, the shimmering waters reflecting a story yet to unfold.

The approach to the Luminous Lake was like treading the line between reality and illusion. With each step, the phosphorescent waters became more brilliant, casting reflections of our past, present, and perhaps, our future.

Elowen hesitated, glancing back at the path from which we came. The intensity of her previous encounter still fresh, her fear was present. Adolwolf, placing a reassuring hand on her shoulder, whispered words of encouragement. They seemed to share an understanding deeper than I had previously comprehended, bound together by a shared past dream. I envied that connection.

Lyria, her eyes shining with a mix of excitement and curiosity, knelt by the water's edge, skimming her fingers across the surface. The water rippled at her touch, and the luminosity surged, painting her face with an ethereal light. She drew back, a look of wonder in her eyes. "The stories of this lake's power were not exaggerated," she exclaimed.

Lysandra watched each of us, her expression inscrutable. "Be wary," she warned, her voice a soft undertone against the gentle lapping of the water. "The lake does not discriminate between pleasurable memories and painful truths. It reflects all, and in that reflection, one might find enlightenment or despair."

Taking a deep breath, I stepped closer, the water pulling me like a magnetic force. The lake, though seemingly calm, had an underlying current of power, a force ancient and immense. I knelt, my fingers barely grazing the surface.

Instantaneously, images began to flicker—fragmented memories of my childhood, my family, moments of joy and sorrow. Then came the shadows, lurking, shifting. But among them was a brighter, radiant force. It took the form of a woman, ethereal and familiar. Mother? Her image was surrounded by a soft light, her face loving and kind.

She whispered, though her lips did not move, *"Rhineheart, your destiny lies not just in reclaiming lost shadows but in understanding the balance between light and darkness. Do not let the shadows consume you. Remember the light."* And then, as swiftly as she had appeared, she vanished, leaving me gasping at the emotional torrent.

I withdrew my hand, staggering back. The weight of her message pressed down on me. What balance was she referring to? I had witnessed the malevolent power of the shadows firsthand. But her words, they hinted at something deeper, more complex.

Lyria, sensing my distress, approached, placing a gentle hand on my shoulder. "Are you alright?" she asked, her eyes full of genuine concern.

"I... I saw her, Lyria. My mother. She had a message for me, but I'm struggling to comprehend its depth."

She nodded, squeezing my shoulder. "The lake reveals truths, but understanding them might take time. We must press on."

The others, having witnessed their own reflections, looked equally moved. Our journey to the Shadow Sanctum was not just about confronting external forces, but also facing our internal demons and understanding our destinies.

The path ahead was uncertain, but one was clear – we were intertwined by fate, and our destinies would be realized together.

As we ventured further into the Forest of Perception, far beyond the solace of the Luminous Lake, the atmosphere became suffocating, both with foliage and an inexplicable sense of anticipation. The trees, gnarled and ancient, seemed to whisper secrets, their leaves rustling with stories of ages past. Their boughs stretched overhead, intertwining in a constellated canopy, filtering the sunlight into sporadic, golden beams that dappled our path.

Adolwolf, seemingly lost in thought, intermittently reached out to touch the bark of a tree or a stray leaf, as if searching for a connection or perhaps an answer. The bond he shared with Elowen, one carved from a dream, felt like an enigma I was desperate to unravel.

Breaking the silence, Elowen softly began, "Do you ever wonder, Rhineheart, if dreams are not just figments of our imagination but gateways to alternate realities?"

I pondered her words, "I used to consider dreams as mere fragments of our subconscious. But after everything we've experienced, I'm starting to believe they're much more."

She nodded; her gaze distant. "In that shared dream, Adolwolf and I discovered a realm where the physical and ethereal blended seamlessly. It was in that dreamscape that we forged our bond, a bond that has clearly transcended into this reality."

Lysandra, eavesdropping on our conversation, "Dreams are said to be reflections of our soul's deepest desires, fears, and memories. But sometimes, they might also be a foretelling, a vision of what's to come or a pathway to a world unknown."

Lyria's eyes sparkled with curiosity. "Then perhaps this journey, this quest to reclaim shadows, was preordained, foreseen in dreams long before we embarked upon it."

While the idea was tantalizing, it was also daunting. Were our steps guided by destiny, or did we have the free will to carve our own path?

Lysandra sensed my contemplation. "While dreams might offer guidance or insights, it's up to us to interpret them and decide our actions. We are not mere puppets of fate."

As we continued forth, the forest began to thin, and in the distance, an ancient stone structure loomed. Cloaked in moss and vines, it appeared as old as time itself. The Silence Sanctum.

"We're close," Lyria whispered, her voice tinged with a mix of excitement and apprehension.

Drawing closer, the air grew colder, and a profound silence deafened us—a silence not of peace, but of anticipation, like the world held its breath awaiting our next move. The entrance to the Sanctum was a massive archway, its stones worn and weathered, guarded by statues of creatures half-human, half-beast, their expressions a mix of sorrow and warning.

Taking a collective breath, we crossed the threshold, unaware that the true test of our courage and determination lay just beyond. The Forest of Perception had been but a prelude.

The interior of the Silence Sanctum was a stark contrast to its forested surroundings. The air was chilled, dense with a heavy, stagnant energy that clung to our skins and seeped into our bones. Torches affixed to the walls burned with a blue flame, casting eerie, ghostly shadows that danced and flickered. The ceiling, lost to darkness, seemed infinitely high, and the walls extended far and wide, leading to corridors branching off into the unknown.

Elowen clutched her pendant, her face pale under the cold luminescence. "This place... it feels like a mausoleum, a resting place for lost souls."

Adolwolf, surveying our surroundings, whispered, "Or perhaps a prison for those who dared challenge the forces that reside here."

Our footsteps echoed ominously as we ventured deeper, the weight of countless eyes watching, gauging our every move. Mysterious symbols and ancient runes were etched into the stone walls, their meanings long lost to time. Yet, an instinctive part of me felt their significance, the power they held.

"We should split up," Lysandra suggested, eyeing the multiple passages that branched from the main hall. "It will increase our chances of finding the heart of this sanctum."

"No," Lyria interjected firmly. "Dividing now, in this labyrinthine abyss, would be folly. We should remain together, for strength lies in unity."

I found myself nodding in agreement. "Lyria is right. The sanctum might be laden with traps or guardians of the shadows. We'll fare better as a united front."

With our course decided, we delved deeper into the heart of the sanctum, drawn inexplicably towards a corridor adorned with a depiction of the moon in its various phases. The path led downwards, a spiral staircase descending into the bowels of the earth.

With every step, the pressure intensified. The weight of the world, or perhaps the countless souls who'd ventured here and never returned, pressed down on us. Whispers of past agonies and regrets seemed to float around, making the journey all the more harrowing.

Hours seemed to pass, and just when the descent felt endless, the staircase opened up to a vast chamber, its enormity dwarfing us. At its center stood a pedestal, upon which lay a dark, shimmering pool, its surface undulating gently. The pool of shadows.

"This is it," Clarissa murmured, her voice a mix of awe and fear. "The crypt of the sanctum, the place where shadows are bound and unbound."

Adolwolf approached cautiously, his eyes never leaving the pool. "We must be cautious. This pool contains not just Clarissa's shadow but the essence of countless others. Disturbing it recklessly might unleash forces we cannot contain."

As we strategized our approach, a voice, melodic yet chilling, echoed through the chamber. "Seeking to reclaim what was lost? Or perhaps, wishing to lose oneself entirely?"

From the shadows, a figure emerged. Ethereal, her form shifting and morphing, her eyes two bottomless voids. The Guardian of Shadows.

Our journey had only just begun.

Her laughter, a haunting cascade, filled the chamber, each note echoing with malevolent glee. Her movements were fluid, almost dance-like, as she circled the pool, her form sometimes blending with the shadows, then re-emerging, her gaze locked onto ours.

"Why have you come here?" she intoned, voice dripping with both curiosity and scorn.

Before anyone could respond, Clarissa stepped forward, resolve evident in her stance. "I seek any remnants of my shadow," she declared, her voice unwavering. "Taken from me, held here against its will."

The Guardian stopped; her amusement evident. "Ah, the lost girl. Who previously, foolishly thought your shadow to be complete after your last encounter with it? Will it make you whole once more?" She laughed again; a sound devoid of warmth. "Shadows are not mere reflections, child. They are desires, regrets, the darkest parts of our souls. And they can and will deceive you. How many times have you thought to have reclaimed your shadow, only to find that it still remains fragmented within each new sanctum?"

Elowen, her brow furrowed, whispered to me, "Rhineheart, there's something more to this guardian. She doesn't merely guard the pool. She is the embodiment of all the shadows contained within."

I nodded, recalling the runes and symbols on the walls of the sanctum. "She is the collective conscience, desires, and fears of all who have ventured here. She is the sanctum."

Lyria, the voice of reason, asked, "What do you want in exchange for Clarissa's shadow?"

The Guardian smirked, her form momentarily flickering, becoming even more translucent. "Ah, the age-old barter. But what can mortals like you offer that I do not already possess?"

Adolwolf stepped forward, his staff glowing dimly. "Knowledge. We offer knowledge of the world above, of things beyond this sanctum. Secrets that even shadows might yearn for."

She paused, intrigued. "Knowledge? A tempting offer. But how do I trust you'll hold your end of the bargain?"

I knew it was my turn. Drawing a deep breath, I said, "By binding my word with magic. A covenant that if broken, the violator will lose their own shadow, becoming one with this sanctum forever."

A hush fell over the chamber. The stakes were high, but so were the rewards. The Guardian seemed to consider our proposal, her form continuously shifting, reflecting the myriad souls she embodied.

Finally, she spoke, "Very well. Impart your knowledge, seal the covenant, and the girl's shadow shall be returned. But remember, betrayal has its price."

The runes on the walls began to glow in response to the covenant we were about to forge. Each symbol represented an ancient pledge, promises made by those who had walked these darkened halls before us.

Adolwolf was the first to step forward, placing his hand over a particular rune, one that signified knowledge. With a low incantation, a spark flew from his fingers to the rune, illuminating it with a deep blue hue. "I offer the knowledge of the art of summoning," he began, "a spell lost to time, one that allows one to call forth beings of another realm."

The Guardian's expression shifted momentarily, a flicker of genuine interest in her otherwise inscrutable visage. "Interesting," she murmured.

Next was Lyria, who gracefully approached a rune depicting a dove in flight. Touching it, a soft golden glow emanated. "I bring knowledge of the Song of Serenity. A melody that can calm even the most turbulent of storms, both in nature and within one's soul."

The chamber seemed to hum softly, as if the very walls were attempting to capture and resonate with the serenade Lyria described.

TEROA

I glanced at Elowen, who gave me a nod of encouragement. Together, we approached a rune intertwined with various elements – fire, water, earth, and air. Placing our hands on it, a vibrant green and amber aura surrounded us. "We offer knowledge of balance," Elowen pronounced, her voice harmonizing with mine. "The understanding of how elements can be combined, not just in spells, but in life, to create harmony."

Lastly, it was Clarissa's turn. She hesitated momentarily but then approached a rune shaped like an intertwining heart and shadow. With a hesitant touch, a radiant silver glow spread. "I offer a memory," her voice was soft, almost a whisper, "of love lost and hope regained. A personal fragment, but one that might provide insight into the emotions that drive mortals."

The Guardian, now a canvas of colors reflecting our offers, looked contemplative. "A diverse array of knowledge. Emotions, balance, art, and serenity. A tempting mosaic indeed."

She waved her hand over the pool, and a shadowy figure – identical to Clarissa, but with a darker demeanor – began to rise, slowly detaching from the inky depths. Clarissa's shadow. The Guardian beckoned, and the shadow hesitated before floating towards her.

With another gesture, the shadow began to move towards Clarissa, who extended her hand, tears glistening in her eyes. But just as the reunion seemed imminent, the Guardian's voice, now icy cold, cut through the tension.

"But remember our deal. If the knowledge offered is false or lacking, the covenant will be broken, and the consequences... severe."

With that ominous warning hanging in the air, we all watched, breaths held, as Clarissa's shadowy fragment melded into her, the young woman shuddering from the reunion. The transformation was immediate. Her posture straightened, and a newfound confidence reflected in her eyes. But was this the final missing piece?

As we prepared to continue beyond the chamber, with our part of the bargain fulfilled, I couldn't help but wonder about the knowledge we'd imparted. Was it enough? And what would the repercussions be if the Guardian deemed our offerings inadequate?

With these unsettling thoughts, we ventured forth. With each step on the ancient stone pathway, I felt the weight of our decisions pressing upon my chest. We had delved into an obscure realm of knowledge, shared secrets once guarded with our lives, and now, the repercussions loomed large and undefined.

Elowen, always keenly perceptive, glanced my way. "Rhineheart, you seem... lost in contemplation."

I met her gaze, the violet depths of her eyes always soothing. "It's the uncertainty," I replied. "We've offered sacred knowledge to an unpredictable entity. I can't help but worry about what that might mean for us."

She gave me a reassuring smile. "We did what we believed was right. For Clarissa. And for the greater balance. Sometimes, that's all we can do."

Clarissa, revitalized with her shadow once more, walked ahead, engrossed in conversation with Adolwolf. He was pointing out certain runes and symbols on the walls, perhaps discussing their significance. She seemed... whole, complete in a way I hadn't observed before. The transformation was both heartening and a stormy reminder of what was at stake.

Lyria's lilting voice broke my observations. "There's a force at play here, stronger than the Guardian or her shadows. I feel it. Like a distant melody, almost familiar yet elusive."

Her words gave me pause. The Songstress of Serenity rarely spoke in vague terms. If she felt something amiss, it was bound to be significant.

"I've felt it too," Elowen admitted. "It's like... threads of a past dream, tugging at the edge of my consciousness."

Adolwolf, overhearing our conversation, "It's possible that this realm resonates with memories, both past and future. Our previous encounters, even those in dreams, might be more connected than we initially thought."

A chilling thought struck me. "Could the Guardian tap into these memories? Extract knowledge or experiences without our consent?"

He pondered for a moment. "It's not entirely implausible. We tread on dangerous grounds, and it's essential we remain vigilant."

An uncanny sense of déjà vu enveloped me, hinting at experiences I was yet to have, and memories that seemed lost in the ether.

Upon rounding a bend, we came across a vast atrium, its ceiling lost in the abyss above. The room was dominated by a massive, spiraled obsidian statue, its design reminiscent of the sigils we'd seen earlier. Around the statue's base were inscriptions, their language ancient and arcane.

Approaching the statue, I felt an almost magnetic pull. Touching its cold surface, a rush of images and sensations overwhelmed me. A shared dream from another time... Elowen and I, facing a menacing darkness, our powers combined in a vibrant dance of light and shadow.

The vision was brief but intense. As I pulled away, I locked eyes with Elowen. The shared recognition was evident.

"We've been here before," she whispered. "In another life, another dream. We've faced the shadows and emerged, not unscathed, but stronger."

The revelation was both comforting and confounding. Our journey had layers we were only beginning to comprehend. Armed with this newfound knowledge, we pressed on, new challenges awaiting our every step.

The deeper we ventured into the Sanctum, the more pronounced the resonance with our collective past became. The walls seemed to vibrate with memories, and the air was full with whispers from long-forgotten conversations. Each footstep seemed to echo with significance, revealing fragments of our shared history.

"I can't shake the feeling," Lyria murmured, her silvery voice tinged with wonder, "that we're not merely retracing our steps, but also paving the way for futures yet unknown."

Elowen nodded, her usually calm demeanor slightly ruffled. "Time behaves differently here. I suspect the lines between past, present, and future are more malleable in this place."

The idea was unsettling. Every choice we made, every word spoken, might ripple through time in unpredictable ways. Adolwolf seemed to relish the opportunity to understand this phenomenon. "We're walking a temporal tightrope," he mused. "The potential for discovery is immense."

I chuckled despite the gravity of our situation. "Only you, Adolwolf, would find excitement in such precariousness."

He grinned, winking conspiratorially. "Every enigma is a door waiting to be opened, my friend."

Yet, it was not the mysteries of time that weighed heaviest on my mind. The force Lyria and Elowen had sensed was growing stronger, its pull more insistent. It beckoned from the depths of the Sanctum, its siren call promising answers and, perhaps, even greater questions.

Guided by this pull, we found ourselves before an enormous portal, its surface shimmering like liquid obsidian. Around its periphery were inscriptions in a language that seemed familiar, yet remained just beyond comprehension.

Adolwolf approached, his fingers tracing the glyphs. "This is ancient, predating most known languages. But I can decipher fragments... 'Boundaries of dreams...' 'Eternal cycle...' 'Awakening...'"

Clarissa, her confidence bolstered since reclaiming her shadow, interjected, "This isn't just a door to another section of the Sanctum. It's a gateway to something... monumental."

As if in response to her words, the portal rippled, and an image began to coalesce. It was a vast, ethereal landscape, punctuated by towering spires of crystal and sprawling forests of silvered trees. At its heart was the Timeless Citadel, its architecture a harmonious blend of nature and artifice. The sky above this realm was a cascade of ever-shifting colors, echoing with the songs of unseen serenades.

Elowen's voice, filled with awe, broke the silence. "The Dreamlands. The realm where all dreams converge, and where realities are born."

Lyria's eyes sparkled with recognition. "A place where thoughts and aspirations take form, where every dreamer has trodden, knowingly or not."

Our path was clear. We had to venture into the Dreamlands, to confront the force that beckoned us and to uncover the deeper mysteries of our intertwined fates. With resolute determination, we stepped through the portal, leaving the shadows behind and embracing a world of endless possibility.

The moment we crossed the threshold, sensations overwhelmed us. It felt as though we were diving into an ocean of emotions, memories, and aspirations. The air pulsed with the very essence of dreams—of humanity's collective hopes and fears, triumphs and regrets.

Our surroundings shifted and morphed, the landscape echoing the fluidity and malleability of the dream realm. As the others observed this shifting reality, I found myself momentarily incapacitated, ensnared in a flood of memories that weren't my own. Whispers of past conversations, fragments of moments long gone, feelings of love, loss, and desire—they all surged within me.

Elowen, sensing my disorientation, offered her hand. Her touch acted as an anchor, and I clung to it, reorienting myself to the present. "The Dreamlands can be...intense," she said gently. "You're experiencing the echo of countless dreamers. It will pass."

With each step, the landscape seemed to solidify, adapting to our presence and collective psyche. We wandered through an orchard of crystalline trees, their leaves shimmering with hues unimaginable in the waking world. Beyond that, we crossed a bridge constructed of interwoven melodies and songs, each note ringing with clarity and emotion.

Adolwolf attempted to document our journey, his quill dancing across the pages. Yet, the ink morphed and shifted as soon as it touched the paper, forming abstract patterns that defied comprehension.

"Seems the laws of this realm aren't conducive to traditional record-keeping," he remarked with a bemused grin.

Clarissa looked more focused; her senses attuned to the rhythm of the Dreamlands. "There's a pull," she whispered. "A beckoning from the Timeless Citadel. That's where we need to go."

The citadel loomed in the distance, an architectural marvel blending seamlessly with the ever-changing environment. It felt ancient yet timeless, holding within its walls the key to the mysteries we sought.

Yet, as we approached, a chilling realization gripped me. The pull I felt wasn't just a mere beckoning. It was a call from someone—or something—intimately familiar, intertwined with my very essence. A presence I'd felt before but couldn't quite place.

"I've been here," I explained, the weight of the revelation pressing down on me. "In dreams long forgotten, in memories I thought were mere figments of imagination."

Elowen cast me a knowing glance. "The Dreamlands are familiar to all, even if most only visit unwittingly. But your connection, Rhineheart, feels deeper, more personal."

We stood before the citadel's grand entrance, poised on the brink of revelations that would undoubtedly reshape our understanding of reality. The shadows we left behind felt like distant memories, replaced by the palpable essence of dreams and the mysteries they held.

With a collective breath, we pushed open the massive doors, stepping into the heart of the Dreamlands and toward the force that had summoned us.

The interior of the citadel was an enigma. Corridors spiraled out in all directions, ceilings stretched infinitely upwards, and walls were adorned with ever-changing murals that depicted dreams of all imaginable natures: some mundane, others surreal, and a few genuinely haunting. The very stone beneath our feet pulsed with a living energy, thrumming softly in sync with the cadence of our heartbeats.

As we delved deeper into its interior, a harmonious chorus swelled around us—soft whispers of long-forgotten lullabies, intertwined with the melodies of dreams yet to come. The very air seemed to hum with the excitement of uncertainty.

Lyria paused suddenly; her keen senses attuned to the nuances of this realm. "There's a resonance here. A familiar energy."

Clarissa nodded; her gaze distant. "Yes, the core of the Dreamlands. It's where dream threads converge and new ones are birthed. It's said to be a source of immense power, but it's also incredibly volatile."

Adolwolf frowned, his scholarly demeanor momentarily replaced by concern. "If that's the case, we must tread carefully. Meddling with the essence of dreams could have unintended consequences."

I felt the pull stronger than ever now, guiding me through the spiraling structure. Rounding a corner, we were met with a vast chamber, bathed in an ethereal green glow. At its center floated a microcosmic model of the universe atop a pedestal, and atop it, a pearlescent orb that pulsated with an inner emerald light, illuminating dream threads that seemed to dance and weave around it.

"I've seen this," I whispered, my voice anxious but unwavering. "In my dreams, long before our journey began. It beckoned to me, urging me to seek it out."

Clarissa approached the orb cautiously. "This is the Pinnacle of Dreams. It's said to hold the essence of every dream ever dreamt and those yet to be dreamed of. Touching it might grant insight or even the power to shape dreams, but it could also ensnare one in an eternal slumber."

I felt a magnetic draw to the orb, an inexplicable yearning to connect with its vast reservoir of memories and emotions. Before I could decide on my next move, a sudden rush of cold air filled the chamber. Emerging from the shadows was a figure, cloaked in tenebrous robes, its face obscured by the darkness.

"Ah, the Dreamwalker returns," it intoned, its voice dripping with a melodic menace. "Did you think you could venture into this realm and not attract the attention of its guardians?"

Adolwolf stepped forward, protective instinct taking over. "Who are you? What do you want?"

The figure chuckled, a sound that sent chills down my spine. "I am the Keeper of the Pinnacle, and you, Dreamwalker, have something I desire."

A feeling of dread settled over me, as memories of past dreams, where the Keeper and I were intertwined in a dance of pursuit and evasion, came flooding back. This entity was no mere guardian; it was an adversary from a time long past. And our confrontation was inevitable.

The Keeper moved closer, the air around her seeming to grow denser and colder with every step. The once harmonious whispers now carried undertones of menace, echoing distorted fragments of memories and shattered dreams.

"I've watched you, Rhineheart," the Keeper purred, addressing me directly. "Navigating through dreams, altering their trajectories, playing god in a realm that you barely comprehend."

"I'm not here to play any games," I responded, meeting her gaze head-on. "I'm here for answers, and to reclaim something that was taken."

The Keeper's laughter echoed through the chamber. "And what might that be? The essence of your shadow? Or perhaps something deeper, a connection lost in the tapestry of dreams?"

I clenched my fists, feeling the weight of the always obscured dream medallion around my neck. "You know why we're here."

"Indeed, I do," the Keeper said, circling us slowly. "But this Pinnacle is not merely a tool for your whims. Every dream it touches, every soul it connects, forms a bond that cannot be easily broken. You meddle with forces beyond your understanding."

Lyria, feeling somewhat diplomatic, attempted to diffuse the tension. "We respect the sanctity of this place. Our intentions are noble. We seek to heal, not harm."

But the Keeper was unyielding. "Noble intentions can pave the way to destruction. You think you can waltz into the core of the Dreamlands, tap into its power, and walk away unscathed?"

Adolwolf, his voice steady, interjected, "We understand the risks. But sometimes, risks must be taken to mend what's broken."

The Keeper's gaze settled on Clarissa. "And you, Shadowless yet delusional. You seem to remember reclaiming your shadow...but have you really? Do you understand the price of reclaiming what you've lost? The balance that will be disrupted?"

Clarissa's eyes shone with a fierce determination. "More than anyone. But I won't stand idly by while my essence is stolen and used for nefarious purposes."

The air grew tense, the pinnacle pulsating more fervently, as if reacting to the charged emotions in the room. The dream threads around it began to sway and intertwine, painting vivid pictures of memories, desires, and fears.

For a moment, everything seemed to blur, and a flood of images washed over me: the joy of my first dreamwalk, the terror of being trapped in a nightmare, the pain of losing a cherished memory. The Pinnacle was connecting with us, merging our dreams and experiences.

It was then that I understood. The Keeper wasn't just a guardian; she was an embodiment of the Dreamlands' consciousness, its protector and judge.

Drawing a deep breath, I stepped forward. "Keeper, we do not wish to disrupt the balance of this realm. But something has been taken from us, something that endangers both our world and the Dreamlands. Let us reclaim it, and we'll leave without further meddling."

The Keeper regarded me for a long moment, her expression unreadable. Then, with a slow nod, she whispered, "Very well, Dreamwalker. But remember, every action has consequences. The Dreamlands will not forget."

As the Keeper faded into the shadows, the Pinnacles glow dimmed slightly, leaving us with a lingering sense of foreboding.

Without the Keeper's looming presence, the chamber regained some semblance of its former tranquility. The luminous threads of the Pinnacle swirled above, filling the void with soft, gentle light. But our group stood silent, each grappling with the weight of the Keeper's words.

"It won't be as simple as we hoped," Lyria finally said, her voice heavy with both concern and determination.

I nodded in agreement. "The Pinnacle is more than just a tool. It's a living, breathing entity, tied to the very fabric of our dreams. We need to tread carefully."

Adolwolf glanced at the Pinnacle, his eyes reflecting the myriad of colors dancing above us. "So, how do we proceed?"

Clarissa, still seemingly lost in thought, quietly said, "We need to connect with the Pinnacle, not dominate it. To understand its desires, its fears. Only then can we hope to fully reclaim my shadow without wreaking havoc or succumbing to illusions of shadow unity."

"And how do we do that?" I asked.

"By merging our consciousness with it," Lyria replied. "It's a risky process, one that demands complete trust and unity among us."

TEROA

Merging with the Pinnacle sounded daunting. Our individual dreams and memories, our very identities, would become intertwined. The boundaries between self and other could blur, perhaps irreversibly.

Adolwolf took a hesitant step forward. "There's no other way?"

Lyria shook her head. "If we force the Pinnacle to relinquish Clarissa's shadow without its consent, the backlash could shatter the Dreamlands. Our worlds would never be the same."

Clarissa, determined, "Then we do it together. As one."

We formed a circle around the pulsating pearlescent orb of the Pinnacle, our hands reaching out to one another. The moment our fingers touched, a jolt of energy surged through us, and the Pinnacle responded in kind, its glow intensifying.

Closing our eyes, we began to let go, surrendering to the pull of the Dreamlands. We dove deeper and deeper, our individual thoughts and memories mingling, our emotions ebbing and flowing as one. It was disorienting, overwhelming, yet strangely liberating.

Time seemed to lose meaning. In the vast expanse of the Dreamlands, we wandered, exploring forgotten memories and reliving cherished moments. But amidst the beauty and wonder, a dark presence lurked—a void, cold and unyielding. It was Clarissa's lost shadow, twisted and corrupted by forces unknown.

Guided by our shared purpose, we approached the void, our combined willpower forming a protective barrier around us. But as we drew closer, the shadow lashed out, its raw power threatening to consume us.

Battling both externally and within, doubts began to creep in. Were we strong enough? Could we truly restore what was lost without destroying the delicate balance of the Dreamlands?

The shadow's influence grew stronger, memories becoming distorted, the line between reality and dream blurring. Just when it seemed all hope was lost, a familiar voice echoed through the chaos.

"Trust in each other. Trust in the journey."

It was the Keeper, her voice a guiding beacon amidst the storm. Rallying together, we channeled our collective strength, surrounding Clarissa's shadow and drawing it closer. Bit by bit, it began to lose its malevolent edge, the darkness slowly receding.

With one final push, we managed to separate the corrupted essence from Clarissa's true shadow, restoring it to its rightful place. As the shadow merged with Clarissa, a brilliant light enveloped us, and the Dreamlands seemed to sing in harmony.

Emerging from the Pinnacle, we found ourselves back in the chamber, the weight of our ordeal evident in our exhausted expressions. But the joy of success, of reclaiming what was lost, radiated from Clarissa's eyes.

"We did it," she whispered, her voice filled with wonder and gratitude.

"Yes, together," I replied, a smile tugging at my lips. "The journey is far from over, but for now, we can revel in this victory."

Chapter 14: Carnival of Shadows

As we began our trek back from the center of the Dreamlands, I couldn't help but reflect on the incredible power of unity and trust. In the face of adversity, when all seemed lost, it was our bond that saw us through. The importance of such connections, the legacies they leave behind, was never clearer to me.

The Dreamlands, with all its mysteries and wonders, held many more challenges and secrets. But for now, we walked side by side, our spirits lifted, ready to face whatever lay ahead.

As the euphoria of the moment began to wane, the sacred geometrical expanse of the Dreamlands stretched out before us. The iridescent corridors seemed to shift and change with each step, leading us deeper into its enigmatic embrace. The very fabric of this world seemed to pulse and breathe, reminding us of its ever-evolving nature.

"We need to be careful," Adolwolf cautioned, his voice echoing slightly in the vastness around us. "The Dreamlands may have yielded to our collective strength once, but it won't take kindly to perceived intruders."

Clarissa nodded, her hand instinctively moving to where her shadow now comfortably rested. "We need to find our way back to the familiar territories, to the realms we know. The deeper we go, the more unpredictable this world becomes."

Lyria's eyes narrowed as she gazed into the distance. "The challenge is that 'familiar' is a fluid concept here. Our perceptions, memories, and emotions shape the Dreamlands. What was once a known path could now be an entirely new terrain."

I felt a pang of uncertainty. Every step in the Dreamlands was like walking on shifting sands, where the only constant was change. "So how do we navigate such a realm?"

Lyria sighed. "By staying connected, grounded. By holding onto the core essence of who we are. The Dreamlands feed on emotions and memories. If we can control ours, we can shape the path ahead."

We moved in tandem, our steps synchronized, our thoughts merging as one. The swirling mists around us began to clear, revealing landscapes that seemed eerily familiar. Visions of childhood homes, long-forgotten playgrounds, and cherished memories came into focus.

"I recognize this," Clarissa murmured, pointing to a quaint little cottage nestled amidst a sea of lavender. "This is where I first learned the art of dream weaving."

Adolwolf chuckled. "And there's the treehouse where I used to dream of our grand adventures."

I smiled at the memory. "Innocent times. Before we realized how vast and intricate the tapestry of dreams really was."

As we journeyed through the interwoven memories, it became evident that our pasts, our histories, were intricately linked. The Dreamlands didn't just reflect individual memories; it melded them, creating shared narratives that bridged gaps between souls.

"Look!" Lyria exclaimed, pointing to a shimmering portal ahead. "That's our way out, the bridge between the core of the Dreamlands and the outer realms."

We quickened our pace, the promise of familiar territory driving us forward. But as we neared the portal, a chilling wind swept through, extinguishing the comforting glow of the Pinnacle and plunging us into darkness.

From the shadows emerged figures, their forms fluid and constantly shifting. They circled us, their whispers growing louder, echoing the doubts and fears that had plagued us throughout our journey.

"You don't belong here," one hissed.

"You can't control the Dreamlands," another taunted.

The figures closed in, their menacing presence overwhelming. But amidst the chaos, a thought resonated clearly in my mind—our unity, our shared purpose, was our strength.

"Stay close," I shouted, pulling the group into a tight circle. "Focus on our bond, on the journey we've undertaken together."

Together, we channeled our collective will, the radiant energy pushing back against the shadowy figures. Slowly, they began to retreat, their forms dissipating like smoke.

The portal ahead pulsed brightly, beckoning us. With renewed determination, we stepped through, leaving the core of the Dreamlands behind.

Emerging on the other side, the familiar landscape of the outer realms greeted us. The weight of our journey, the trials and tribulations, seemed to lift, replaced by a sense of accomplishment and unity.

"We did it," Lyria whispered, her voice tinged with awe.

"Yes," I replied, gazing at the horizon. "But our journey is far from over. The Dreamlands have shown us the power of unity and the importance of leaving a lasting legacy. Now, it's up to us to uphold it."

The landscape of the outer realms, while more familiar, held its own mystique. Unlike the pulsating core of the Dreamlands, this was a realm of stark contrasts—where dense forests bordered vast deserts and towering mountain ranges gave way to sprawling meadows. It was a place where reality and dreams harmonized, each influencing the other but in ways that maintained perpetual balance.

Clarissa, her shadow now fully integrated, moved with a newfound grace, her steps confident and purposeful. "The Dreamlands may be unpredictable, but there's a beauty to its unpredictability, a reminder of the vastness of human emotion and memory."

Adolwolf nodded in agreement. "It's a reflection of us—our hopes, fears, desires, regrets. And the more we journey through it, the more we understand ourselves."

I gazed at the horizon, a myriad of colors painting the sky. The outer realms might have been more predictable, but it was in the Dreamlands that true self-discovery took place. "The journey within is often more challenging than the journey without," I mused aloud.

Lyria looked at me, a knowing smile on her face. "And yet, it's the journey within that truly defines us."

As we moved forward, the terrain started to change. The vibrant meadows transformed into a dense, almost impenetrable forest. The trees stood tall, their canopies blotting out the sun, casting long, sharpened shadows on the ground.

"The Forest of Forgotten Dreams," Clarissa whispered, a hint of trepidation in her voice. "It's said that those who enter are confronted with memories they've tried to bury, dreams they've abandoned."

Adolwolf frowned, concern evident in his eyes. "Then we must tread carefully. Facing forgotten memories can be more daunting than any physical challenge."

Lyria paused, taking a deep breath. "But it's also an opportunity for healing, for reconciliation with our past."

I nodded. "Every challenge in the Dreamlands is an opportunity for growth. We'll face whatever memories arise, together."

Steeling ourselves, we ventured into the forest. Almost immediately, the atmosphere changed. The air grew ominous with emotion, each step unearthing fragments of long-buried memories.

Images flashed before my eyes—of laughter and joy, of heartbreak and loss, of dreams nurtured and dreams discarded. Emotions swelled within me, threatening to overwhelm. But as I looked around, I saw the same determination in the eyes of my companions. We were in this together, our bond unbreakable.

Hours, or perhaps years—time held little meaning in these confusing realms—passed as we navigated the forest. Each of us faced our own challenges, our own memories. But with every step, with every memory confronted, we grew stronger.

Finally, the dense canopy began to thin, and the oppressive weight of the forest lifted. Ahead, a clearing emerged, bathed in the soft glow of the setting sun.

We stepped into the clearing, a sense of peace and contentment converging on us. The challenges of the Forest of Forgotten Dreams had been daunting, but they had also been healing. We had faced our past, embraced our memories, and emerged stronger.

Looking around, I realized that the journey through the Dreamlands had permanently changed us all. We were no longer just travelers; we were legendary dreamweavers, shaping and being shaped by the realms around us.

Within the clearing, the soft chirping of unseen critters provided a gentle melody. As the sun began its descent, a gentle mist began to rise from the ground, enveloping the surroundings in an almost surreal haze.

Lyria approached a large, moss-covered stone in the center of the clearing, her fingers gently touching its rough surface. "This," she began, her voice soft and reverent, "is the Stone of Remembrances."

As we drew closer, the stone began to emit a soft, luminescent glow. The patterns and symbols etched into it, previously hidden, now became visible, dancing and shifting as if alive.

Adolwolf studied the markings with intense curiosity. "This stone is older than any memory, and so it remembers everything. Every dream, every emotion, every soul that has traversed the Dreamlands."

I placed my hand on the stone, and a rush of memories surged through me. My mind raced with images of my childhood. The small cottage by the lake, the stories told at bedtime. The fleeting feelings of security before it was all taken away.

"It's a reminder," Clarissa said, her voice filled with solace, "that our individual journeys are but a single thread in the vast tapestry of existence. We are all interconnected, our dreams and memories shaping and being shaped by one another."

There was a profound truth to her words. In the vast expanse of the Dreamlands, where thoughts and emotions took tangible form, it was evident how deeply interwoven our lives truly were. Every action, every emotion, left a mark, rippling through the dreamscape.

We spent many stars by the Stone of Remembrances. It was a place of reflection, of understanding, of connection.

When the time came to leave, we did so with heavy hearts but with a renewed sense of purpose. The challenges we had faced, the memories we had uncovered, had all led to this moment. Our journey was no longer just about navigating the unpredictable landscapes of the Dreamlands; it was about understanding the intricate web of dreams and memories that bound us all.

As we ventured unwittingly onward, the line between dream and reality began to blur. But one thing was clear: we were not mere travelers in this realm. We were dreamweavers, shaping the very fabric of the Dreamlands with every step we took. And with that power came a responsibility, a duty to protect and nurture this fragile realm.

The journey through the Dreamlands was not linear, as nothing in this realm adhered to the strict constructs of time or space. Sometimes, it felt as though we'd stepped into memories from our distant past, or even glimpses of futures yet unwoven. The landscapes shifted seamlessly from dense forests to vast deserts, from frozen tundras to vibrant meadows. The constancy was its unpredictability.

However, with Lyria as our guide and the Pinnacle as our anchor, we moved forward with determination. Along our path, we encountered dreamers — lost souls adrift in their own nightmares or blissfully ensnared in their deepest desires. With Clarissa's newfound abilities and our collective will, we managed to guide many back to the path of wakefulness, granting them a respite from their ceaseless dreaming.

One evening, as the crimson and gold hues of the sky painted the horizon, we found ourselves by a vast, tranquil ice sheet. Its surface mirrored the twilight perfectly, making it hard to discern where the land ended and the ice began.

We set up camp by the mountainous ice sheet, the rhythmic whipping of the icy air creating a peaceful ambiance. As night deepened, Lyria began singing a hauntingly beautiful melody, her voice echoing across the frozen waters.

"Lyria," I murmured, drawing closer to her, "that song... it feels ancient, filled with longing."

She gave me a melancholic smile. "It's a song from my earliest memories, passed down through generations in the Dreamlands. It speaks of a time when dreams and reality were one, a harmonious symphony. It's a reminder of what we're fighting for."

Sitting there, with the shimmering ice as our backdrop and Lyria's song filling the air, a deep sense of camaraderie was shared between us. Despite our disparate backgrounds and the constant challenges we'd faced, our shared experiences had forged an unbreakable bond.

But as the night deepened, a peculiar phenomenon began to unfold. The ice, previously serene, started to crack and churn. Whispers, soft and insistent, emanated from its frozen depths. Lyria's song faltered, and her face turned frozen.

Clarissa, sensing the impending danger, whispered, "We're not alone."

From the center of the massive ice sheet, a colossal shadow began to rise, its form indistinct and constantly shifting. It was as if the darkest essence of the Dreamlands had coalesced into a singular entity, its intentions unreadable.

Adolwolf stepped forward, brandishing his ethereal blade. "Whatever you are, we mean you no harm. But we will defend ourselves if necessary."

The entity remained silent, its shadowy fingers reaching out, probing and testing our resolve.

As its power washed over us, I felt a pull, a beckoning. It was a call to remember, to understand, to awaken.

As the entity's incomprehensible grasp inched closer, our group tightened into a protective circle, each of us drawing strength from one another. The Dreamlands might be unfamiliar terrain, but our shared purpose, the importance of reclaiming balance, grounded us.

"My shadow, it is still not whole!" whispered Clarissa, her voice quivering with a mix of confusion and anticipation. "It's calling to me. It wants to merge, but it's bound, restrained by something far more sinister."

Lyria's eyes darkened with understanding. "This is not just any entity; it's the Guardian of Forgotten Dreams. It safeguards those dreams too powerful, too dangerous to be let loose. Your shadow's union with such potent dreams might have rendered it too powerful."

I gritted my teeth, trying to fight the oppressive aura that the Guardian exuded. My memories of contemplation and epiphany, every experience and lesson I'd learned in my time both in the Waking and Dream realms, surged forth, guiding my actions. "We cannot back down now," I declared, voice firm. "We're here to free every ensnared shadow, including Clarissa's."

Adolwolf, his blade glinting with a silvery light, nodded in agreement. "We stand together, as one."

As if responding to our unwavering determination, the Guardian let out a spine tingling, mournful wail. The very air around beneath us vibrated, filled with an overwhelming sense of loss and longing. The Guardian wasn't just a mere protector; it was the embodiment of abandoned hopes, of dreams forsaken and forgotten.

The shadowy tendrils grew more desperate in their approach, almost pleading. But intertwined with that desperation was a palpable anger, a fierce protectiveness over the dreams it had sworn to guard.

Lyria, her voice resonant with power and ancient knowledge, began to chant. It was a counter-song to her earlier lullaby, a melody of release, understanding, and reconciliation. "Hear me, Guardian! We seek not to destroy but to restore. To bring balance where there is chaos, light where there's shadow."

The Guardian's wailing intensified, echoing Lyria's chant in a sorrowful duet. The two voices, one filled with millennia of wisdom, the other with timeless grief, intertwined, creating a harmony that permeated the very fabric of the Dreamlands.

I felt it before I saw it – a softening, a subtle shift in the Guardian's stance. The aggressive tendrils began to retract, replaced by gentler, more curious extensions. It seemed to be... listening.

Clarissa stepped forward, extending a hand towards the Guardian. "I understand your pain, your duty. But my shadow is a part of me. I need it to be whole again."

As if sensing the sincerity in her plea, the Guardian hesitated momentarily before slowly, tentatively, releasing a wisp of shadow towards her. The wisp danced in the air before merging with Clarissa, who gasped, overwhelmed by the flood of emotions and memories.

As the union completed, the Guardian, its duty fulfilled, began to dissolve, its form blending with the tranquil waters of the lake created by the melting of the ice sheet, leaving behind an undisturbed, serene expanse.

We stood there, by the lakeside, absorbing the magnitude of what had just transpired. The Guardian might have been a formidable entity, but at its core, it was a sentinel of dreams, a protector of hopes.

"We're one step closer," Clarissa whispered, her voice filled with gratitude.

With the Guardian's dissolution, a pathway materialized across the lake — stepping stones made of luminescent moonstone, gleaming with an inner light. A bridge between realms, perhaps? Our group moved towards it instinctively.

Each step on the stones felt like a memory — moments of happiness, pain, laughter, and tears. It was as if the Dreamlands itself were sharing its history with us, reminding us of the importance of our quest.

"Does anyone else feel... lighter?" Adolwolf mused aloud, looking at his hand as if seeing it anew.

Lyria smiled, "The Guardian's touch was not purely combative. In its own way, it was showing us the weight of lost dreams, the power of abandoned hopes. Now that we've faced it, we've been cleansed, in a sense."

I felt it too. The weight of my own forgotten aspirations seemed to have been lifted. It was a surreal feeling — to be in a place that could confront you with your deepest regrets, yet also offer redemption.

The last stone led to the shores of another realm within the Dreamlands. Verdant meadows stretched out before us, dotted with groves of violet-barked trees bearing luminescent fruits. It was both alien and familiar, like a half-remembered dream from childhood.

As we ventured further, we found ourselves in a clearing where dreamers, in various states of wakefulness, sat in clusters. Some were engrossed in their own dreams, their expressions flickering between elation, sadness, and contemplation. Others were in deep conversation, their words a melodic blend of countless languages, both known and unknown.

A tall, ethereal figure approached us. Dressed in robes made of starlight, they emanated an aura of ageless wisdom. "Welcome, Travelers of the Waking Realm," they intoned, voice echoing with the sound of a gentle night's breeze. "I am Elandrial, The Philosopher of Dreams. You've ventured far from your own realm, crossing barriers few dare to tread."

Clarissa, with newfound confidence, stepped forward, "Elandrial, we come in search of lost shadows, fragments of ourselves that have been torn from us. And from that the means to maintain a perpetual balance with this world and the next. Can you guide us?"

Elandrial considered her for a moment, their gaze piercing, yet not unkind. "Many come to the Dreamlands seeking what they've lost, be it hope, love, or memories. Yet, shadows are unique, for they represent both self and the absence of self. Your journey has only just begun."

A shiver ran down my spine. The Dreamlands were vast, and we had faced but one of its many challenges. But Elandrial's words also hinted at hope, a promise of guidance.

"We are prepared," I said, determination strengthening my voice. "Guide us, Elandrial. Help us restore what was taken."

The Philosopher of Dreams nodded slowly, "Very well. But remember, in the Dreamlands, the line between perception and illusion blurs. Trust in your companions, rely on your instincts, and most importantly, believe in the power of your own dreams."

With those cryptic words, Elandrial gestured towards a grove, where the trees bore fruit resembling shimmering orbs. "Each orb is a dream, a world unto itself. To find the shadows, you must delve deeper, navigating the dreams of countless souls. Only then might you find the path to what you seek."

With the Dreamlands opening its secrets to us and Elandrial's guidance, we were one step closer to understanding the elusive nature of shadows — and perhaps, our own selves.

The grove was a mesmerizing sight. Each tree bore dozens of orbs, and every one was a gateway to a dream. It was a breathtaking testament to the infinite nature of the human psyche.

Lyria plucked an orb from a tree, holding it up to her eyes. It pulsed gently, emitting a soft glow that illuminated her face with an ever-changing play of colors. "Each dream is unique, a manifestation of one's deepest desires, fears, and memories. Some are whimsical, while others carry the weight of centuries."

She turned the orb in her hand, and for a fleeting moment, we glimpsed a snowy landscape, vast and pristine, populated by shadows of creatures long extinct. "This," she whispered, "is someone's escape. A place where they find solace from the challenges of their waking life."

Adolwolf reached for another orb, drawn to its fiery glow. As he touched it, the clearing echoed with the haunting sound of a violin, its melody filled with a deep yearning. He looked at us, his eyes shimmering with unshed tears. "It's... it's a memory of my mother. She played this for me when I was a child."

It was evident that the Dreamlands didn't just contain the dreams of those currently asleep. It was a repository of dreams from time immemorial. Adolwolf's contact with the orb had bridged the gap between his conscious self and a deeply buried memory.

I tentatively reached out, touching an orb that pulsed with a cool, aquamarine light. The world around me faded, and I was submerged in a vast ocean. Around me, majestic sea creatures swam gracefully, their bioluminescent forms casting eerie lights in the dark depths. Above me I saw the constellation of Pisces, and as I observed, those stars swirled and formed into an an ocean brimming with life. It was a tranquil dream, untainted by fear, where the dreamer found peace in the embrace of the waters of life.

As I pulled back, I realized that each dream was an intimate peek into someone's soul. It felt like an immense responsibility to tread within these orbs. Elandrial had said we needed to navigate these dreams. But how? The sheer number of orbs was overwhelming.

Clarissa's voice, filled with determination, broke through my thoughts. "We can't possibly explore each dream. We need a way to narrow down our search. Elandrial, how do we discern which dreams might lead us to our shadows?"

Elandrial replied, "The dreams linked to your shadows will resonate with your very being. You must open yourself to the energies of the grove, let your intuition guide you. The path may not be linear; dreams are not bound by the same laws as the waking reality."

Taking a deep breath, we closed our eyes, allowing the ambient energy of the grove to envelop us. Moments turned to minutes, and soon, an intrinsic pull directed me towards a specific tree. The orbs it bore were different — darker, their insides swirling like a tempest.

"This is it," I whispered, feeling the resonance deep within. "Our shadows are somewhere beyond these dreams."

With a collective sense of purpose, we reached out to touch the dark orbs. The world around us melted away, and we plunged into a dream like no other, seeking the fragments of ourselves lost within the infinite expanse of the Dreamlands.

The dreamworld that greeted us was not one singular plane but a complex mosaic of intertwined visions, a complex constellation of emotions and thoughts. Beneath our feet, a cobblestone path unraveled, winding and twisting around itself like a serpent, while above us, a crimson sky loomed, flecked with shards of silvery lightning.

The atmosphere was peppered with tension, every gust of wind echoing with whispers and fleeting memories. To the left, a carnival with blindingly bright lights beckoned, the haunting strains of a calliope playing in the distance. To the right, an ancient forest stood silent, its trees gnarled and contorted, as if writhing in agony.

Lyria's gaze was unwavering, fixed on the carnival. "That's where we need to go. I can feel it. The shadows are drawn to places of strong emotions, and there's an evident sense of nostalgia and yearning emanating from there."

Without waiting for our response, she set off toward the carnival. We followed, the ground shifting and undulating beneath us as if it were alive, reacting to our thoughts and fears. As we neared the entrance, a grotesque clown with an unsettling wide grin barred our way.

"Welcome to the Carnival of Lost Souls," he intoned, his voice dripping with malice. "To enter, you must offer a memory."

Clarissa, determined and brave, stepped forward. "What kind of memory?"

"One that you hold dear," the clown replied, his eyes gleaming with mischief. "A moment that shaped you."

She hesitated only for a moment before recounting the day her younger brother had been born, how she'd felt an overwhelming rush of protective love, how his tiny hand had wrapped around her finger. The clown listened intently, his grin never wavering. Once she finished, he motioned for us to proceed.

One by one, we all shared memories: Adolwolf spoke of a childhood summer, playing by a serene lake. Lyria described a tender moment with her grandmother, learning the ancient songs of her people. I recalled my first venture into the Dreamlands, the awe and wonder it inspired in me.

With our admissions complete, the clown bowed deeply, his grin now genuinely warm, if still unnerving. "You may enter. But remember, the carnival is not just a place but a state of mind. Beware the illusions."

Stepping inside, the atmosphere was at once jovial and somber. Everywhere we looked, dreamers were lost in their own worlds: some laughing merrily on carousels, others staring desolately into funhouse mirrors that distorted and twisted their reflections.

In the midst of it all, shadows flitted and danced, occasionally merging with a dreamer or simply observing from a distance. The challenge now was to discern which shadows belonged to us.

Lyria, with her innate sensitivity to such energies, led the way. She moved with a purpose, dodging carnival games and attractions, until she halted before a grand tent bearing the sign, "The Theater of Reflection."

"This is it," she declared, pushing aside the tent's flap. "Our collective shadows, and that of humanity, reside within."

As we entered, a vast, ornate theater unveiled itself. A single spotlight illuminated the stage, and as we took our seats, the curtains rose, revealing a series of vignettes, each a pivotal moment in our lives. And behind each tableau, the sinister silhouettes of our shadows lurked, their forms ever-shifting, tethered to our very souls.

Our quest to reclaim our lost fragments had led us here, to confront our pasts and, in doing so, shape our futures.

The vignettes moved with an ethereal fluidity, moments of joy, pain, discovery, and loss melding together. Each scene was a vivid and esoteric reminder of the human capacity for a spectrum of emotions, the play of light and shadow on the stage echoing the duality within our souls.

In one tableau, Clarissa danced with a shadowy figure resembling her younger self, mirroring the emotions she'd felt upon her brother's birth. In another, Lyria sat cross-legged, surrounded by shadows mimicking her elders, listening intently to a song that seemed to resonate through the very fabric of the theater.

Adolwolf's shadow was more elusive. It flitted about, laughing and singing, embodying the carefree days by the lake he had recounted. But as the scene transitioned, a darker moment took the spotlight, revealing a young Adolwolf crying alone in a corner. The juxtaposition was a stark reminder of life's complexities.

Then it was my turn. The stage transformed into a surreal landscape, capturing my initial foray into the Dreamlands. Mountains soared into skies painted with twilight hues, and rivers gleamed like liquid silver. My younger self stood at the precipice of a vast chasm, looking equal parts awed and terrified. The shadow behind me was almost imperceptible, a mere wisp, signifying the early days of my understanding of this realm.

As the scenes played out, an underlying thread became reiterated: these were our formative experiences, the moments that had shaped our very identities.

A sudden hush enveloped the theater. The curtains drew closed momentarily, only to reveal a final, collective scene. All our shadows converged on stage, a maelstrom of dark energies, their forms constantly shifting, intermingling. In their midst stood a solitary figure, neither entirely shadow nor light, its face obscured. It was Morphean, whom we had not encountered for what seemed like ages. He gazed upon us and opened a portal in front of us, center stage. "You all must now enter into this portal and weave your dreams upon the great tapestry of the universe. With your challenges now complete, let us celebrate in your newfound wisdom tempered through compassion and reason.

Chapter 15: The Great Tapestry

As we had come to learn, the realm of dreams is not one of constancy. It morphs, it breathes; it is as fickle as the dreams that shape it. As the radiant light dissipated from Morpheans portal, we found ourselves on an iridescent expanse, stretching endlessly in every direction. Above us, the sky pulsed with unseen hues, each shade representing a dream that had been dreamt, or perhaps, was in the process of being dreamt.

Beside me, Lyria looked around, her eyes wide with wonder. "It's magnificent," she breathed, her voice carrying a note of awe.

Before us, suspended in the infinite expanse, was a vast, intricate weave. It pulsed with life, each thread representing a dream, a memory, a possibility. The Tapestry seemed alive, constantly shifting and changing as new dreams were added and old ones faded away.

As we drew closer, we realized that the Tapestry was not complete. There were gaps, tears, and frayed edges, representing dreams unfulfilled, memories forgotten, and possibilities never realized.

The Pinnacles words echoed in my mind, "Only by weaving your shadows into it can you hope to reclaim what was lost and shape the dreams of countless others."

But how? The magnitude of the task was overwhelming. How could we, mere mortals, hope to impact this vast expanse of collective consciousness?

But as I gazed at the Tapestry, a realization dawned. It was not about changing the entirety, but about adding our own threads, our dreams, our memories, and our hopes to the weave. By doing so, we would maintain perpetual balance, but also leave a lasting legacy, a part of ourselves in the very fabric of the Dreamlands.

Resolute, we approached the Tapestry, ready to begin this seemingly final phase. But as we neared, an ominous presence made itself known. A colossal figure made of starlight, far larger and more menacing than any we had encountered before, emerged from the depths of the Tapestry.

"You dare to approach the fabric of the Dreamlands?" it boomed, its voice a cacophony of countless voices and planetary sounds. "What do you hope to achieve?"

"I am Rhineheart," I began, stepping forward slightly and meeting the gaze of the gargantuan sentinel, "And we seek to mend and add to the Great Tapestry. To reclaim perpetual balance, to add our own dreams and hopes to the fabric of the collective consciousness."

The guardian, a swirling entity of starlight, studied us intently, its form constantly shifting, making it hard to discern where it truly began or ended. "Many have tried, few have succeeded. The Dreamlands do not take kindly to interference, even from its own children."

Adolwolf, always the voice of reason and wisdom, asked, "What is the price for this interference, and can it be negotiated?"

"Price? There's always a price," the guardian murmured, its voice taking on a soft, melancholic tone. "The price is the essence of your true self, your core memories and experiences. You may weave your story into the Tapestry, but you also relinquish a part of yourselves to it. Those memories, once woven, are set in the records of time, never to be altered."

Lyria's voice quivered but held firm. "Is it a sacrifice or an offering? There's a difference."

"Both," responded the guardian. "An offering to the dreams of the future, a sacrifice of the personal recollections that make you who you are."

A heavy silence settled over our group. The implications of the guardian's words were immense. To give up our most cherished memories, our defining moments, in pursuit of a greater legacy, was a daunting prospect.

As I pondered the gravity of our journey, the Seeker of Truth, my own shadow, whispered in my ear, "Remember, Rhineheart, the essence of this mission has always been about legacy. It's about the importance of our place in the vast weave of dreams and memories."

I nodded, taking a deep breath. "We understand the weight of our actions, and we are prepared to offer a part of ourselves to the Tapestry."

The guardian regarded us for a moment, then slowly retreated, merging with the vast weave before us. "Very well," it intoned. "Approach the Tapestry and begin your weaving."

One by one, we stepped forward, our fingers grazing the vibrant threads. As we touched the Tapestry, memories—our joys, our heartbreaks, our defining moments—flowed from us, intertwining with the existing weave. The sensation was both painful and cathartic, a simultaneous loss and gain.

Hours, or perhaps eons, seemed to pass, but there was no relativity here. Finally, as the last thread of our collective memories found its place, we stepped back, exhausted but fulfilled.

The Tapestry now bore our mark, our stories forever enshrined in the Dreamlands. As we turned to leave, the guardian reappeared, its form softer, more defined. "You have done well. Your stories are now a part of the eternal dream. Go forth, knowing you have left an indelible mark on the fabric of existence."

The Dreamlands, though vast and infinite, were made of stories. Every weave in the Tapestry represented countless tales, memories, and legacies. As we moved away from the Great Tapestry, the weight of our decision and the realization of our permanent mark on this eternal landscape filled me with a sense of humility.

In this newfound peace, the journey back to our starting point seemed less arduous. The paths, which had previously twisted and turned unpredictably, now felt welcoming, guiding us smoothly.

"We've changed," Lyria mused aloud, her fingers tracing an intricate pattern in the air, a remnant of the weaving we had done. "Not just the Tapestry, but us. In giving away our memories, we've reshaped ourselves too."

Adolwolf glanced at her, his ageless eyes reflecting deep understanding. "We have. Every decision, every action, changes us in ways we can't even begin to comprehend. The Dreamlands merely made it tangible."

I found myself nodding. "It's like the ripples in a pond. One small stone can create waves that stretch far and wide."

Our journey was met with fewer obstacles. The once-hostile entities of the Dreamlands now seemed almost curious, approaching us with tentative interest. In giving our memories to the Tapestry, we had become a part of the Dreamlands' story, and the very essence of this realm now recognized us as its own.

We camped for a time by a luminescent pond, its waters shimmering with memories of dreams past. As I sat there, lost in thought, a soft voice broke my reverie. It was the Seeker of Truth, my shadow, now more distinct, its form solidifying.

"You did well, Rhineheart," it said. "But remember, the Tapestry is ever-evolving, ever-changing. What you've given is eternal, but it's only a part of a much larger narrative."

"I know," I replied, gazing at the reflections in the water. "But it's a start. A legacy."

The Seeker smiled, a strange sight on a shadow. "Yes, a legacy. But legacies aren't just about the past. They're also about the future. What you leave behind is important, but so is what you choose to do moving forward."

As we prepared to continue our journey, I realized that the Dreamlands had not just been a destination but a teacher. We had learned about sacrifice, about legacy, and about our own places in the grand tapestry of existence.

But, as the Seeker had reminded me, our story was far from over. There were still many paths to explore, many dreams to witness, and many more tales to add to our own ever-evolving narrative. The Dreamlands awaited, and we were ready to embrace its mysteries anew.

Author Biography

Reid Abraxas emerges onto the literary scene with the enchanting depth and complexity of a seasoned storyteller, despite being a newcomer to the world of published authors. Born and raised in an obscured area known more for its historical architecture than its literary pursuits, Reid's fascination with the interplay between the seen and unseen, the tangible and intangible, began at an early age. With a background steeped in the study of classical literature and philosophy among ancient forests and whispering rivers, Reid's approach to storytelling is both methodical and whimsical.

Made in the USA
Monee, IL
06 April 2024